A Nagging Feeling

A slug popped up gravel not ten feet ahead of Slocum. He growled and reined his horse, at a surprised and sudden gallop, back toward a low cluster of paloverde. It was a bad place to hide, but in this desert it was the only cover for miles.

He grabbed his rifle, leapt off the gelding while it was still at a gallop, and dived for the scraggly trees, rolling when he hit the ground. And only once he was in the cover of the paloverde and settled did he check to see where his horse had gone. It was galloping off into the distance, reins flying.

His eyes squinted against the Arizona sun, and he searched the far-off canyon rim. Whoever was up there hadn't fired again, so far as he could tell. And then he saw a tiny puff of dust, moving out from behind a tall pile of boulders, moving south.

"You lousy piece a crud," he muttered. "Why'd you take a potshot at me when you were just gonna ride off?"

It was that sonofabitch who'd swiped his horse. Slocum was as sure of it as he was of his name. The bastard had circled back and fired at him, and now he figured that Slocum was horseless and couldn't follow him . . .

HOT ON THE TRAIL

JOVE BOOKS, NEW YORK

HOT ON THE TRAIL

A Jove Book / published by arrangement with the author

PRINTING HISTORY
Jove edition / May 2002

Copyright © 2002 by Penguin Putnam Inc.

Visit our website at
www.penguinputnam.com

ISBN: 0-515-13295-0

A JOVE BOOK®
Jove Books are published by The Berkley Publishing Group, a division of Penguin Putnam Inc., 375 Hudson Street, New York, New York 10014.
JOVE and the "J" design are trademarks belonging to Penguin Putnam Inc.

PRINTED IN THE UNITED STATES OF AMERICA

10 9 8 7 6 5 4 3 2 1

1

In the thin, bluish shade of a boulder high above the broad valley floor, Hector Quintana lay flat on his belly, his rifle at his shoulder, his binoculars before him. Sweat trickled along his temples and ran slowly down his nose as he waited, his eye on the tiny dot of a solitary rider moving toward him on the dusty road below.

He picked up the binoculars for the fifth time in as many minutes, wiped the sweat from his eyes with the back of his gloved hand, and took another look.

He frowned. Still too far to make out the face. Still too far to see if it was truly one of those murdering sons of bitches.

He lay the glasses down carefully and wiped at his face again, then the back of his neck. His stomach was buzzing, fluttering. The tension of it, he supposed. He'd tracked that notch-hoofed sorrel of Guardado's over half the territory. Right into Pozo Artesiano, he'd followed the horse's tracks, and right out again, going south, always going south. Right now, he was well over the border and into Mexico.

Not that it mattered much where he killed the bastard. Hector didn't care. He just wanted Guardado dead.

One long week since he'd found Ramona dead. One long week since he'd found her body, thick with buzzing flies, lying outside what was left of his smouldering little rancho.

He closed his eyes, willing the image away. Not now. Now wasn't the time to remember, to have his eyes clouded with tears. There had been three of them, three sets of tracks. He had buried his Ramona as best he could, and then he had started after her murderers.

He followed them down into Hobbsville, which was nothing more than a wide spot in the road, but it was in Hobbsville that he learned the names of the men he was following.

Punk Alvarez, the short fat one, according to the man at the falling-down livery, rode a gray gelding that toed in with the right front. Lando Reese, a "mean piece of business," rode a bay gelding, the only horse of the three that didn't leave a unique hoofprint. And Gordo Guardado, the tall fat one (as opposed to Alvarez, Quintana assumed), rode a sorrel with a notched hoof.

Well, not the hoof, exactly, although Quintana thought of it that way. The stableman said that the horse's shoe was damaged, had a big ding gone out of it. He'd offered to throw a new shoe on there, but Guardado was in too much of a hurry.

Apparently, Guardado had been in a big hurry for the whole of the past week.

The riders had split up outside Pozo Artesiano, and Quintana had been vastly disappointed. He'd squatted on his heels, studying the tracks while his own horse, Tico, stood lazily behind him, and then he had stood up, swearing a blue streak. His outburst had spooked Tico, and he had to apologize to the horse.

And so he'd chosen to dog Guardado's trail for no particular reason, except that it was arguably the easiest to follow.

The men had been moving south, then east, and now that they had split up, Hector hadn't changed his plan. There was only one canyon Guardado could travel through without cutting ten miles to the east or fourteen to the west.

Hector knew this country. He knew that it was possible for him and Tico to hotfoot it up and around Gordo Guardado, and quite literally cut him off at the pass.

So now he waited for that tiny sorrel speck to draw closer. He waited for his chance to kill.

Revenge is almost at hand, Ramona, he thought as his hand went to the binoculars again.

He brushed away the sweat once more and held the binoculars to his eyes. He squinted. He pulled his head back from the eyepieces, shook it, then pressed the eyepieces home again.

Why, this man wasn't fat, wasn't somebody that would pick up the nickname of Gordo at all! The horse was sorrel, all right, but the lean man riding him wasn't even Mexican, so far as he could tell. Hector watched as the rider came slowly nearer and nearer. A tall man, by the look of it, a man with dark hair and a hard face . . .

"Well, I'll be a badger's smelly backside!" Quintana breathed.

Abruptly dropping the binoculars, he stood straight up, abandoning any and all hope of cover. He pressed the rifle's butt against his shoulder, took aim, and fired.

When the slug popped up gravel not ten feet ahead of him, Slocum simultaneously growled, "Shit!" and reined his horse, at a surprised and sudden gallop, back toward a low cluster of paloverde. It was a bad spot to hide, but in this desolate place it was the only cover for miles.

He grabbed his rifle, leapt off the gelding while it was still at a gallop, and dived for the scraggly trees, rolling when he hit the ground. And only once he was in the cover of the paloverde and settled did he check to see where his horse had gone. Unfortunately, it was galloping off into the distance, reins flying.

Great, just great. It'd probably take him a week to find the damn thing, if it didn't run itself to death first.

Eyes squinted against the bright Arizona sun, he searched the far-off canyon rim. Whoever was up there hadn't fired again, so far as he could tell. The sound of the first shot hadn't even reached him until he was halfway to the paloverde.

He couldn't see anyone, couldn't see a damn thing but the rocks that formed the crumbling cliff side. His rifle was already at his shoulder, but he reached down and brought out his Colt, setting it in the dust in front of him just in case.

And then he saw a tiny puff of dust, moving out from behind a tall pile of boulders, heading south along the rim.

Slocum let out a disgusted whoosh of air. "You lousy piece'a crud," he muttered. "Why'd you take a potshot at me when you were just gonna ride off?"

It was that son of a bitch who'd swiped his horse. Slocum was as sure of it as he was of his name. The bastard had circled back and fired at him, and now he figured that Slocum was horseless and couldn't follow him. Lousy prick. He was just going to ride off as pretty as you please.

"My ass, he is," Slocum grumbled. He dusted off his britches, holstered his Colt, and, his Winchester swinging from his hand, stood up and started along the trail of the galloping—and vanished—sorrel.

By the time he'd walked about three-quarters of a mile—with no horse in sight—he noticed a plume of dust coming toward him from the south. Instinctively, he made ready to dive for cover, but found none. This

stretch of the wide canyon floor was a good mile wide
as well as flat and sere, with not so much as a stunted
creosote bush or clump of bunch grass that a man could
hide behind.

Cursing, Slocum turned to the side in order to make
himself a narrower target, set his feet wide apart, cocked
his Winchester, and nestled it into the curve of his shoulder, eye sighting down the steel barrel. He stood his
ground.

But then he began to make out the forms within the
dust roil. Not one horse, but two. And one horse was
riderless.

His sorrel?

Slowly, he lowered the rifle, muttering, "What the devil . . . ?"

The rider, whose face was still obscured by swirling
dust, slowed as he approached. When he was about
thirty feet out, he suddenly stopped the horses and
stepped down to the ground. Slocum had his rifle halfway to his shoulder again before the man, his fist full
of reins, walked forward out of the dust cloud, swept off
his hat, and slapped it across his thigh with a loud pop.
He was tall and dark and lean, with exotic features punc-
tuated by startling blue eyes.

"Slocum, you lousy sonofabitch!" he said gleefully.
"What the hell are you doin' out here?"

Slocum's brows both popped up. "Hector?" A smile
blossomed across his face. "Hector Quintana, as I live
and breathe! I thought you were dead!"

The two men slapped each other's shoulders, laughing, and Hector said, "I thought the same about you, old
friend. Heard you were killed up in Utah. Course, another fella told me you were up on the Platte River when
you bought the farm."

Slocum grinned. "Well, I was up there all right. Both
places. But I'm pretty tough to kill. I heard you ran into

some Mex soldiers that sent you to Jesus."

Hector shrugged. "An exaggeration. They only sent me to Chihuahua."

Slocum chuckled. By God, it was good to see Hector again! What had it been, seven years, eight? And was he still riding the same horse?

Slocum said, "Was that you, shootin' at me from up there?" He tipped his head toward the cliffs.

Hector snugged his hat back on his head. " 'Fraid so. Wanted to get you stopped, and it was too far to holler. Hell, I didn't know you'd go divin' for cover and lose your horse."

Slocum grunted. Hector was a pretty fair hand, but sometimes he just did things that didn't make any sense. Taking potshots at people, for instance. Slocum had always written it off as a result of Hector's rather confused heritage, since Hector was a quarter Yuma Indian, a quarter Mexican, a quarter Irish, and a quarter Dutch. Slocum figured a background like that was enough to scramble any man's thinking. He also figured Hector's family reunions must sound like the destruction of the Tower of Babel.

Hector gave his ear a scratch. "Well, leastwise I brung him back." He handed over the reins. "What I want to know is where the hell you picked him up, because I've been trackin' him for about a week."

Slocum's ears perked up. "Trackin' this horse, or trackin' the weasel-brained son of a bitch who was ridin' him?"

"The last one," Hector said with a little nod. "Gordo Guardado."

"Well, get in line," Slocum said as he swung up on the sorrel.

Hector followed suit. They reined the horses around and started down the canyon again at a walk. Both animals were lathered, the sorrel from his race and Hector's mount from chasing him.

Hector said, "If you don't mind my askin', what are you after him for?"

"Son of a bitch stole my horse in Pozo Artesiano," Slocum said with a certain degree of disgust. "Stole him right off the rail in front of Muy Malo's place."

Hector's face lit up with a grin. "Paolo 'Muy Malo' San Francisco? He still run the whorehouse up there?"

"Yup. He's not runnin' a horse-holdin' business though. He was pretty damn quick to point that out to me."

Hector nodded. "I wondered why you weren't ridin' one of them loud-colored Palouse horses. I'd have recognized you a lot faster. As it was, I damn near blew your head off."

Slocum didn't argue with him. Hector was a keen shot. His ability as a sniper was on a par with Slocum's own. Slocum said, "That isn't the same bay you were ridin' last time, is it?" And when Hector nodded, Slocum added, "Christ, Hector, that was what? Eight years ago?"

" 'Bout that," Hector said, patting the bay's neck. "Unlike you, Slocum, I figure when you find a good one, keep him. Had my Tico since he was foaled. Owned his mama out in California."

It would have been obvious to a blind man that Hector was smitten with that horse. Slocum couldn't say that he blamed him. Tico was a nice one, all right, and he said so, adding, "That is, if you like those plain-colored horses."

Hector gave a smirk.

Slocum asked, "Why are you out after Guardado?"

"My Ramona," Hector said after a moment, and it came out thick. "He killed my Ramona."

Slowly, Slocum said, "I'm right sorry, Hector, right sorry. I didn't know you'd married." He couldn't think of anything else to say, and he sure wasn't going to ask any questions, at least not at the moment. Judging by Hector's face, he'd loved her deeply, and Guardado had made a bad job of it.

But, just a tad testily, Hector said, "I didn't wed up with nobody, Slocum. Ramona was my camel. You know, left from when the surveyors was here back in the fifties? She was one'a the last ones. Maybe the very last. Why, she was as gentle as they come. She'd lip sugar candy right outta your hand. And then Guardado had his pals come along and they shot her. The bastards tied her to the fence and used her for target practice, it looked like. I counted twenty-six slug holes. Burnt my place, too," he added as an afterthought.

Now, Slocum didn't know much about camels. He knew that the Army had tried using them about thirty years ago and then had given up, turning most of them loose in the desert. Nature, mean-spirited cowboys, and hungry Indians had taken care of almost all of them pretty quickly. Frankly, he was amazed that one could have survived this long. Maybe it was a second-generation beast, he didn't know. He didn't suppose Hector did, either.

But his initial reaction, which was to laugh at the thought of Hector having taken in such an ungainly, cantankerous critter, was quickly offset by the way in which Hector spoke of it. He supposed a man could take a good liking to a camel the same as he'd take a liking to a dog. The same as Slocum himself had taken to a few horses over the years and Hector had taken to Tico.

Why, back in '76, hadn't Slocum tracked down Toffy Goodman—and eventually shot him dead—after he'd stolen, then ridden to death, that good leopard chestnut mare of his? It wasn't all that long ago that he'd shot a man, then lashed him to a rock and printed the words "Horse Killer" in blood on it, after the scabrous son of a bitch shot Slocum's good gelding horse.

In fact, several men had died because they'd taken too much of a shine to horses Slocum was riding at the time. And to his mind, there was nobody worse than a god-damned horse killer. He reckoned, therefore, that if a feller was fond of camels, well, camel killer ran a close second.

He didn't see it, but then, he wasn't Hector Quintana. He said, "Sorry, Hector. I mean that."

2

They picked up their pace after the horses had cooled out, and by nightfall they had narrowed the gap between themselves and Guardado to exactly thirty yards and gaining, give or take a yard or two.

Guardado, who had no idea that he was being followed and therefore believed he had no need to hurry, much less be secretive, had made camp at the base of a cliff. He had tethered Slocum's horse in the low scrub about ten yards from his little fire, and he was just setting his beans to soak when Slocum popped up, his rifle ready.

Slocum and Hector had snuck in from upwind, but when the Appy saw Slocum he lifted his head high and gave a nicker of recognition. Guardado suddenly looked up, then lunged to his feet, slopping half the beans in the fire. He had his pistol most of the way clear of its holster when Hector, who'd crept around to his far side, cocked his pistol and said, "Not so fast, you stinkin' pig squirt."

"Ease that gun out, Gordo," Slocum called.

Guardado did.

"That's the way. Now toss it on the ground."

11

The outlaw's gun raised a small cloud of dust when it hit. He was well over six feet, with a big beer belly that pooched over his belt and a face like an axe blade padded between two pillows. He also looked scared, Slocum thought.

All things considered, he'd be an idiot to look any other way.

"How you know my name, señor?" Guardado asked in a trembling voice.

Slocum didn't bother to answer. He moved forward through the dry weeds, not caring that he made a racket. He'd been creeping in those damned weed and bushes for so long, trying to be quiet, that it felt good to make a lot of noise.

"Easy, Creole," he said when he got as far as his horse. He quickly glanced at the gelding, giving him a cursory once-over. He looked fine enough. Didn't look mistreated. Slocum wouldn't know for sure until he actually got his hands on the horse, but first things first.

Hector was closing from the other side and he looked mad enough to just plug Guardado, no questions asked. Although no words had been exchanged between the two, Guardado seemed keenly aware of Hector's disposition, and babbled, "I have no money, señors! I am a poor man! You can check my saddlebags!"

"I don't know about that, Gordo," Slocum said, and the man's head swiveled toward him. "You've got my horse. And those are my saddlebags you're askin' me to check, you moron."

Guardado gulped, and Slocum could practically see the gears turning in his head. "I—it was a mistake, señor!" he yelped. "I only borrowed him, I swear it!"

Slocum and Hector had both stepped into the little clearing by this time, and Slocum said, "Borrowed him? You wanna explain that, Gordo?"

"Maybe I didn't borrow him," Guardado backpedaled.

"Maybe it was an accident? I-I was drunk. I got on the first horse. I thought it was mine." Guardado gave a small shrug, as if to say that everybody made mistakes, didn't they, but Slocum wasn't buying it.

"Musta been pretty damn drunk to mistake a loud-colored Appaloosa for that sorrel piece'a shit you were riding."

Guardado shook his head slowly. "Oh, I was very drunk, señor. It was the mescal. It was bad. I was very sick."

"Not as sick as you're gonna be," Hector said, and Guardado's head twisted back toward him.

"I have only stolen the one horse, señor!" said Guardado, and his voice broke, just a little. "Does it take two men to come after me for one little horse?"

"Torcher," said Hector in a low tone. "Barn burner. House lighter." His voice ground down to a growl. "Camel killer."

Again, Guardado gulped. "The camel?" he practically squeaked. "That was a mistake," he said. "An accident!"

Hector's frown deepened. "Your pistols accidentally went off twenty-six times? You accidentally set fire to my place, you sick badger's butt?" Hector was looking itchier and itchier, and Slocum figured he'd best do something to distract him.

He said, "Hector, pat Gordo down. Make sure he's not carryin' any surprises, and then let's get some rope on him."

"Señor!" protested Guardado, his eyes wild. He bolted and lunged toward the brush, but Hector caught him by the arm, mid-stride, and yanked him back. Guardado fell and sat down hard on the rocky ground.

"Calm down," Slocum said. "Ain't gonna hang you."

Hector, standing over Guardado, angrily asked, "Why the hell not?"

Slocum rolled his eyes. "Think about it, Hector."

Hector stood there simmering for a half a minute, and then he seemed to relax a mite.

"Get up," Hector said gruffly to the exceedingly nervous Guardado, who was beginning to twitch. Once he was standing, Hector started patting down Guardado's legs and checking his boots for weapons. After he'd tossed a knife with an eight-inch blade and a pocket gun to the side, he called, "All right."

"Rope," said Slocum.

"Gladly," replied Hector.

"*Mierda,*" muttered Guardado.

After they led their horses into camp and got them settled, Hector took a stab at preparing supper while Slocum checked over Creole. He was a handy gelding, and nice-sized at just over fifteen hands. He was also what they called a chestnut leopard, which meant that his base color was white, and he was covered with deep chestnut spots that ranged in size from the thumbprint ones that freckled his legs and face, to the fist-sized spots that blanketed his body. Slocum had traded a black stud with a snowflake blanket for him about a year back, and he had never regretted it.

As he ran his hands carefully up and down the Appy's legs, feeling for anything out of the ordinary, it occurred to him that he had bad luck with chestnut leopards. He'd had the one stolen and ridden to death a few years back. But then, he'd had just about every kind and color of pony stolen from him at one time or another.

He wasn't sure whether to chalk this up to Guardado's being an awful good judge of horseflesh—along with half the goddamned territories—or just plain bad luck.

Maybe it was both. Good luck and good judgment on Slocum's part to find a quality mount, and bad luck when a horse thief—who was just as good a judge of horseflesh—came along and swiped it.

He walked Creole around to confirm his initial opinion that the horse was fine, just fine. And Guardado hadn't spurred him bloody or cut his mouth. Slocum would give him that, he supposed, but he was still mad as hell that the horse had gone missing in the first place.

"Biscuits're ready," Hector called.

Slocum muttered a gruff "Yeah" in reply and tied Creole to the picket line again. Giving him a last pat on the neck, he moseyed over to Hector and the fire.

Hector had done quite a job on Guardado. He'd bound the fat bandit hand and foot, and when Guardado had finally come to realize that Slocum and Hector weren't gong to perform an impromptu hanging—and started mouthing off—Hector had gagged him as well, using a pair of Guardado's own dirty socks.

"Stinkin' camel killer," Hector muttered to himself as Slocum knelt down across the fire from him. "Oughta tie him to a damn fence and shoot him twenty-six goddamn times. What kind of a person goes around doin' such cruelties?"

Gordo Guardado said something into his gag, but it came out, "Mrph mrph."

"Shut up," growled Hector. "Animal torturer."

Slocum, who had already gingerly taken a piping hot biscuit from the pan, said, "Beans ready, too?"

Hector picked up the spoon and smashed a bean against the side of the pot. "Bubblin' and ready," he said. "I oughta take these beans and pour them down the front'a your britches, that's what I oughta do," he said to Guardado.

Since the beans were boiling pretty fast and furious, Slocum said, "Now, calm down, Hector. We want him goin' to his maker in his original condition, not with his privates cooked."

Guardado was silent, but his eyes were bigger.

"Won't be soon enough for me," Hector muttered, and

slid the lid off a skillet he'd had sitting off at the side. "This is pretty fair ham, Slocum." He forked a thick slice onto his own plate, then Slocum's. "You're travelin' rich."

Slocum scootched back from the fire and sat. Although it had cooled down some, it was still hot enough out here, even after dark, without huddling over a flame. Setting his plate aside, he poured himself a cup of coffee, then dug into his supper.

"Ain't so rich," Slocum said at last. "Last of my roll. I was headed over Tucson way—got a job there—when this asshole swiped Creole."

He tipped his head toward Guardado, who was staring forlornly at their plates. A small line of drool leaked from beneath his woolen gag.

"Tucson?" asked Hector. "What kind of a job, if you don't mind my askin'."

Slocum nodded, and around another mouthful of ham, he said, "Salty Nelson wired me. Got himself a little trouble with rustlers."

Hector snorted. "Must be pretty big trouble if he called you in. Salty Nelson, Salty Nelson . . . Wasn't he the feller what you got tangled up with on Cutthroat Creek back in '71?"

Slocum gulped his coffee down and poured out another cup. It was awful good grub, better than he could have cooked up out of what he had in his pack. He said, "Christ, you got some memory, Hector! But no, that was Horseface Nelson. You know, I believe this is the best coffee I've had in a coon's age. What the hell'd you do to it?"

Hector shrugged. "Just a little scrape of nutmeg. I tote quite a few spices in my pack. Keeps the trail from gettin' boring, you know? And if I run outta meat, well, I can spice up a rattlesnake to taste like just about anything. Anything but snake, that is. I hate snake."

He'd done something to the beans, too, but Slocum was too busy eating to comment. At last, he set his plate down, reached in his pocket for his fixings, and began to roll a quirlie.

Hector reached for Slocum's plate, asking, "You done?"

Slocum waved him away. "Just takin' a breather between courses. That's good grub, Hector. Got a mind to ask you to ride on over to Salty's place with me. If you'd keep on doin' the cookin' that is," he added with a grin.

Hector pursed his lips. "No, amigo. There were two more'a these snakes that come by my place, murderin' and torchin'. I ain't gonna quit until I get the other two."

He looked pretty set on it, but Slocum tried again. "Hector, you can't just go and shoot 'em. Now, this boy's on his way to the gallows, as sure as I'm sittin' here. But it's 'cause he thieved a horse, not 'cause of your camel. It pains me to say it, but the law don't count that as a crime. If you manage to track down the other two and do what you're sayin', you'll end up hanged yourself. And just between me and you, I'd sure hate to see that happen."

But Hector's expression didn't change, and Slocum could see that he hadn't moved him, not one whit.

"I loved that camel, Slocum," Hector said. "Loved her like most fellers'll love a favorite hound. Why, she come to me all beat up by time and the desert. Just limped up by my corral lookin' for water with her head hangin', waitin' to die." He stared at his hands for a moment, then looked up.

"Now, I may be a jackass," he went on, "but I ain't so much of one that I don't know when an animal's in distress, and I sure ain't one to go killin' any critter I figure can be saved. I nursed her back from the edge, Slocum. And I didn't do it so that some shit-for-brains drifter and his buddies could just tie her up where she couldn't get away, and shoot at her till she died. A tame pet, she was! She'd follow you around and everything! Used to nose my pockets, she did, lookin' for treats."

Hector tossed Guardado a murderous look. "These scrofulous coyotes don't deserve to live."

Well, Slocum had to agree with him. In his experience, there were just some fellas that didn't warrant the air it took up to keep them breathing, and these three appeared to be in that bunch.

But he gave his head a shake and said, "Not arguin' with you, Hector. It was a low thing, what they did. I'm just sayin' that if you track 'em down and kill 'em, the way you're plannin', you'll be just as low in the eyes of the law."

"So be it, then," Hector said.

Slocum lit his quirlie and shook out the match. He knew Hector well enough not to quibble with him, at least right at the moment. It'd take most of tomorrow to haul Guardado back to Pozo Artesiano, and he figured he could talk Hector out of a couple of revenge killings on the way in.

At least, he hoped he could. He'd lost a great many friends lately, and he didn't want to count Hector among the lost.

Around his quirlie, he said, "You reckon we should feed old Gordo, over there?"

Hector stared at the fire. "You do it, Slocum. I'm liable to choke him white."

3

The next day found them on the trail back to Pozo Artesiano. Slocum, who was happily back aboard Creole, led Guardado's sorrel with him atop it. Hector wouldn't even touch Guardado's lead rope.

By noon, Slocum had again tried to convince Hector to give up the chase and had gotten exactly nowhere. He had, however, learned the names of the other two men Hector was chasing. There was Punk Alvarez, who Slocum learned was short and fat and rode a gray.

That information didn't do much to whittle down the odds of finding Alvarez, even when Hector told him the man's horse toed in a tad with his right front foot. Half the male population of the West was short, a fair percentage of them were fat, and horses could be traded.

He didn't mention any of this, however, because the second name that Hector gave him stopped him cold.

Lando Reese.

If there was ever a cheating, lying, murderous son of the devil, it was Lando. Plug ugly, too. Slocum had tangled with Lando Reese just once, and that once was enough to last him a lifetime. Two years back, when he'd heard that Lando had been drowned down in Mex-

19

ico City, he'd bought every mother's son in the place a whiskey. That had been in the Quarter Horse Saloon up in Cheyenne, which was a big establishment, and that act of largesse had wiped out his purse. It was worth it, though. He was that celebratory.

It occurred to him that there were quite a few men that he'd like to see horsewhipped, if not hanged or just plain killed. Lando Reese was one of them. Tom Stipkin, too, the man who'd made a fool of him up in Montana, and then killed a woman and her kid on his way out of town. Ike Milk, Jefferson Smith, Leonard Peavy . . . The list went on and on.

But most of them were dead already. Nat Plum, Mel Farmer, Mickey "The Mick" O'Toole, "Big Daddy" O'Hara . . . That list was a good bit longer. There were a few that were question marks, though, like Cole Strait. Strait had been an officer in the Army of the South when Slocum was just a corporal assigned to his unit.

He'd been assigned sniper duty, and was up in a tree one night, up high, watching the too-near enemy lines, when he overheard Strait talking with his men. And what they were talking about sure wasn't anything to do with winning the war.

Slocum had turned them in, and after the court-martial, when they were being loaded on the train in chains, Strait had sworn to get "that sniveling Slocum." Slocum had taken it with a grain of salt. After all, they were going to be hanged by the Confederacy in a week.

But Strait and his men had somehow managed to break out of prison a few days after they got there. The other two had been accounted for in the years since, but Cole Strait had just plain vanished, so far as Slocum knew.

Well, hell. He was probably long dead, too. Slocum always remembered him, though. Strait had given Slocum his first taste of humankind's duplicity. He'd admired the man. But when he heard him plotting to steal the South's gold, steal money right out of the hands of Jefferson Davis and the tatty band of men following his cause . . .

He shook his head. Why he should be thinking about Cole Strait at this moment was beyond him. There were more important men to tend to.

"You're after Lando Reese?" he asked Hector in disbelief.

"You know him?"

"I know him, all right," replied Slocum, who suddenly realized that all the muscles in his back were as tense as fiddle strings. He wasn't sure if Lando Reese or Cole Strait had strung them so tight, but he willed himself to relax.

He said, "I had me a share in a mine about four years back, and Lando Reese murdered my partner. I took out after him, but I lost him halfway to California. I heard he'd got killed. Sorry to hear I heard wrong."

Gordo Guardado, who had said less than four words the whole time they'd been on the trail, suddenly laughed and said, "He is a hard one to kill, that Lando. I think he will dance on your graves, señors!"

Hector twisted in his saddle and barked, "And I'm gonna piss on yours, you son of a bitch."

Slocum knew that Hector would do it, too, and didn't say a word. He didn't know which was worse—the times when Hector's Yuma part came out, or the ones where his Irish side stepped to the fore. Actually, they were pretty much interchangeable, except the Irish one was more bloodthirsty. Also verbose. He couldn't speak for the Mexican and Dutch parts, although for all he knew the Dutch bit of Hector could have been pretty wild and bloodthirsty, too.

He didn't know much about Dutch.

It was late afternoon when they finally rode into Pozo

Artesiano, and by that time a fair-sized dust storm was whipping up. They stopped at the sheriff's office first thing, and despite the wind, Slocum insisted that they leave the door open so that he could watch Creole.

Once burned, twice shy—that was Slocum's motto, and he'd be damned if he'd leave him tied to a rail for some other idiot to steal.

"Delighted to take him off your hands, Slocum," Bill Ploughshare said as he turned the key on a scowling Guardado. "Believe we'd have 'bout enough to hang him even if he hadn't swiped your pony. And I'm glad you decided to bring him in alive, Quintana. I would've hated to put paper out on you."

Slocum filled out the papers and, with Hector, split a small reward for bringing Gordo Guardado to justice. As they left the sheriff's office, Slocum clinked his half—fifty dollars in gold—in his palm. "Nice surprise," he said.

Hector pocketed his. "I told you he was bad," he muttered, and stepped up on his horse.

A short ride down the main street found them at Juan Garza's livery stable, where they were greeted by Juan himself.

"Hey, Slocum!" he called over the wind. "I see you find your measles-spotted horse!" He opened the barn door wide and motioned them inside. "You find him fast, too," he said with a sagacious nod as Slocum and Hector rode inside and dismounted. "The man who steals him, is he still breathing?"

"Breathing and in the hands of Bill Ploughshare," Slocum said. He patted Creole's neck.

"Ah," said Garza. "Then he will not breathe much longer, I think." He turned toward Hector, with whom he was apparently already acquainted, for the two of them exchanged nods. "That is one of the three you seek, is it not, Señor Quintana?"

Hector nodded his head yes, but Slocum snorted. "Hector, you musta really made the rounds while you were in town."

"That I did." Hector led Tico, a smart bay, into an empty box stall and began to work at his cinch. "And I'm headin' out first thing in the morning after them two others. That'a boy, Tico," he murmured to his horse. "We'll get you some oats in a minute."

Garza ran to latch the door, which the wind was flapping noisily on its leather hinges.

Slocum led Creole into the next stall. "Well, you're gonna have a devil of a time of it, that's all I can say. That howler out there has already blown any tracks they left practically to South America."

"Farther, I think," piped up Juan Garza, who had closed the door and was wiping dust and grit from his face with a once-white handkerchief. One corner of it still was. "It is a bad one to come so early." He gave a cursory rub at his drooping mustache, then tucked the handkerchief in his back pocket. "Full grain and a rub-down, Slocum, like always?"

Slocum slid his saddle off Creole and swung it up next to Hector's, on the top rail of the stalls' common partition. "Just like usual, Juan. And remember to stay clear of his tickle spot."

Garza nodded.

"Me, too," said Hector, without waiting to be asked. He unbuckled his horse's bridle and slipped it off with a soft *clunk* of the bit on Tico's teeth. "Tickle spot?"

Slocum rested a hand on Creole's side, high and almost back to the hip. "He doesn't take to metal touchin' him right here. Ask Juan."

Garza said, "*Sí.* Nice of you to warn me this time, Slocum, but I think I would remember. I just got the wall fixed."

Slocum already had Creole's bridle off and was latch-ing the stall door behind him. He'd tried everything he could think of to talk Hector out of this fool's errand, and the dust storm was the clincher. There was no way in hell that Hector would catch up to those two now, and no way even a gifted tracker like Hector could trail them. But Slocum'd be damned if he'd bring the subject up again. Hector's stubborn streak had him worn down to a nub.

If he wanted to go wandering around out there, so be it.

Slocum reached into his pocket and fingered the gold coins. "Hector," he announced. "It seems to my mind that blood money needs spendin' in a big hurry."

"Agreed," said Hector, his face serious. "Not good to hang onto it any longer than a feller's got to."

"What do you say we go get us some supper, then we take ourselves over to Muy Malo's for the evening? Maybe book a couple'a gals for the whole night."

Hector's mouth loosened into a smile at last. "My sentiments exactly."

"Señors?" said Juan Garza. He held out his hand and slowly shook his head like a disapproving schoolmarm. "If you do not mind so much, would you pay for the horses' keep before you spend all your money on food and cerveza and women?"

Two hours and a good meal later, Slocum was drowsing happily in the arms of a buxom and chubby-cheeked soiled dove by the name of Pearl. Still stark naked, she was curled in the crook of his arm, one finger alternately curling rings in his chest hair or tracing the tracks of old scars along his torso.

Hector had chosen a flamboyant redhead called Scotch Marie, and hadn't been heard from since. Slocum hoped he was trying to spend all his money.

He knew he was.

Pearl's hand fluttered up to caress his cheek. "You awake, Slocum?" she asked.

He chuckled. "I see you quit callin' me 'Cowboy.' "

He felt her give a little shrug. "Feller who can do it twice in an hour—and do it real nice, not all quick and rabbitty—deserves to be called by his name, I'm thinkin'."

Slocum felt himself stir, and in his head the cash register went off again. *Ka-ching!*

Grinning, he turned toward Pearl. "How 'bout another one on old Gordo?"

Her brow furrowed. "On who? I don't do no three-ways, Slocum, not unless I get paid awful good."

"It's only a figure of speech, Pearlie-girl," he said, and placed his hand gently on her white belly, then slid it lower to brush her pale pubic curls. "There's just me here."

The corners of her mouth rose into a slow smile, and she reached for his stiffening cock at the same moment that he slid his fingers between her outer lips, to the silken skin beneath, and began to slowly pet her.

"Slocum," she whispered as she pushed against petting fingers, "you sure know how to put a gal in the mood." Her hand began to work on him, trailing up and down, circling the head, palming the silky droplet of moisture from the tip and smoothing it over him.

"You ain't so bad yourself, Pearl," he murmured, and dipped his head to take her nipple in his mouth.

Moments later, he mounted her and slowly slid his length easily inside her. She uttered a little sigh, and he began to move. She moved with him, raising her buttocks and tilting her hips in time with his every thrust.

He rode her long and leisurely, bringing her almost to the point of orgasm several times, then backing off while she pleaded with him to finish it. He wasn't ready yet, though. He was enjoying the feel of her, the feel of being inside her—her tight walls hugging him, pulling at him—and her short nails raking his back and arms.

At one point he raised himself up on his hands so that he could look down at her as she writhed beneath him, her full breasts trembling with every movement, her eyes closed, neck craned back, her mouth open as she gasped for air.

"Slocum," she managed to get out. "Please!"

It was time, he supposed. He began to quicken the pace of his thrusts, driving deeper and deeper, pulling back farther, until each stroke was as long and fast as he could make it.

She came within seconds, freezing into a statue with her hips up off the bed and her mouth open wide, and Slocum held her until he felt her body begin to melt back and become pliant again. Then he whispered, "We're not done yet, Pearl."

Never breaking contact with her, he sat up, pulled her legs up over his shoulders, then rose to his knees, lifting her hips along with him.

When she blinked in surprise, he said, "Hang on, baby," and began to thrust again. After a moment, she locked her heels behind his head and began to meet him once more, and this time he pounded into her over and over, letting out all the stops, pushing as deep and hard as he could.

Pearl's hands gripped the bedclothes, pulled them into knots. Her round breasts bobbled and shook with his thrusts. She began to make a high, keening sound, and Slocum figured it was time to let that itch in his loins come to a full boil.

Actually, by this time he was so wound up that he didn't have much choice in the matter.

He felt himself getting bigger. For a moment it seemed he would strain Pearl's insides to the breaking point, and the moment he thought it, he exploded.

Pearl did, too, freezing once again while Slocum pumped into her again and again, until all his seed was spilled.

After a moment, he slowly eased her down to the mattress again. She opened her eyes and groaned, "Holy shit."

He lowered himself down beside her, kissed one of her pale pink nipples, and said, "Pearlie, I think you'd best let me sleep for a bit."

She rolled over, cuddling along his side. "How long, honey?" she purred like a cat in the cream.

"Oh, I don't think I'll be ready for another half hour, anyway," he said, his eyes closed.

"Holy shit," she whispered again.

At about four in the morning, Slocum wandered downstairs. He'd rented Pearl for the night, but she was dead to the world and he was ravenous. He hoped Paolo "Muy Malo" San Francisco had a plate of fried chicken—or something equally tasty—set aside in the kitchen.

There was nobody downstairs. That parlor was dark and the piano was silent. Even whorehouses had to close up shop sometime, he supposed.

He groped his way down the back hall in the darkness. Light fanned from beneath the kitchen door, however, and he opened it with a grin. Maybe Muy Malo had been thinking about chicken, too.

But it was Hector, dressed in his britches, socks, gunbelt, and nothing else, who greeted Slocum.

"Top of the evenin' to you," he said, raising the hand that wasn't full of a roast pork sandwich. He shoved the roast and a carving knife toward Slocum, and then the bread plate. "Butter's on the counter," he added before he took another gargantuan bite.

A pork sandwich would do just fine, Slocum thought,

and his mouth was watering already. He began to hack off a thick slice of pork.

"Been thinkin'," Hector said, once he'd swallowed.

" 'Bout what?" Slocum set to slicing the bread.

"You know damn well about what," Hector said. " 'Bout trailing them boys."

Slocum, trying not to appear too interested, slathered butter on both slices, then sat down at the table, facing Hector. He nestled the pork on the bread, dusted it with salt, then pepper, and put the lid on it. He lifted the sandwich in both hands. With it poised inches from his mouth, he asked, "Come to any conclusions?"

Hector tipped his head slightly, as if to say that he had given in to nature and common sense, although grudgingly. "I ain't gonna try to follow 'em," he said. "Hell, they could be anywhere."

Slocum, whose mouth was full of pork and bread— and it was damn fine pork and bread, too, if you asked him—simply nodded. After a moment he swallowed and said, "That's the way I see it, too. You feel like takin' a ride over to Tucson with me?"

"To Salty Nelson's?"

"Yup. Unless you're of a mind to get back home and start rebuildin' your place."

Hector shook his head sadly. "No rush. Didn't have no livestock anyway. Just Ramona. And Tico, of course."

Slocum cocked a brow. "Hector, how can you have a place and not have so much as a chicken on it, let alone a steer or two?"

Hector shrugged. "Well, I won it in a poker game a few years back. The sneaky son of a bitch I won it off of beat me down there and sold off his cattle and let all the hands go before I had a chance to take over the ranch. Just never got around to replacin' 'em, that's all."

Slocum chuckled. "You beat everything, Hector, you know that?"

"Been told. Ain't that sandwich kinda dry with nothin' to wash it down?"

Slocum, who had taken another bite, nodded. "Good, though," he said around a full mouth.

Hector snagged a pitcher and two glasses off the counter. He sniffed at the pitcher's contents, then smiled.

"Buttermilk," he said, and proceeded to pour the glasses full. "Always liked buttermilk." He shoved a glass at Slocum, who took it readily. "You givin' that gal of yours much more time to catch up on her beauty sleep?"

Slocum grinned and swallowed. "Not hardly," he said before he took a long gulp of buttermilk. "Not hardly at all."

4

Two days later, Lando Reese reined in his bay outside the narrow pass that opened into Devil's Canyon. He took off his hat and waved it twice, wide and theatrical, up toward the boulders on the rim, then settled it back on his head and waited, watching expectantly.

In less than a minute, a hatless head popped up, then an arm, and then the arm waved a broad-brimmed hat back at him.

Lando kneed his horse forward again at a walk, and into the mouth of the long, narrow pass. The streaked and striated limestone walls—white and pink and yellow and sandy brown—towered a good fifty feet above him, and rose up close enough that he could have touched both of them if he'd held his arms out wide.

He continued down this pass—sometimes so narrow that his knees and stirrups brushed the walls, sometimes wide enough that three men could have ridden abreast—for perhaps three hundred yards, and then it suddenly opened out into an enormous, grassy canyon.

Devil's Canyon had been misnamed, Lando thought, probably by some joker just like him. Somebody who wanted to scare off anybody nosy enough to go snooping. Of course, the narrow pass that led to it probably gave the devil's own time to any man chasing elusive Apache, who had used the canyon at one time or another. The battered, scattered skeletons he'd crunched over in the pass—both human and horse—and the scrapes and scratches marring the soft limestone attested to arrows having been fired from above. Quite a few arrows, and over a long period of time, if he was any judge.

But there were no Apache now, only Cole Strait's men. And the cattle, of course. Their lows had greeted him when he was only halfway down the pass. They milled before him in the bright midday sun: shorthorn steers, mostly, with a cow and calf here and there. They were all fat and glossy from grazing on knee-high grass, and there were at least a hundred head of them. That was his guess, anyway. Cole should be about ready to push them down into Mexico, to market.

The sound of approaching hooves turned Lando's attention to the east. Two riders loped toward him and reined their horses in just a few yards away. The first rider, hand on the butt of his sidearm, eyed him and said, "Lando Reese?"

The second just sat back and grinned at him.

To the first, Lando said, "None other." To the second, he said, "How goes it, Tinker?"

"Goes fine, goes fine," Tinker said as his left eye wandered lazily up, then out to the side. Lando had always figured that Tinker ought to wear a patch over the damn thing. It was disconcerting as hell. However, Tinker Reese wasn't a man you made suggestions to.

The first rider said, "You vouch for him, Tinker?"

Grinning, Tinker said, "Hell, Bob. I oughta know my own brother, hadn't I?"

*   *   *

That evening, Slocum and Hector made camp in the mountains just southwest of Tucson. By Slocum's reckoning, they ought to make it down to Salty Nelson's ranch, the Lazy D, by early afternoon of the next day. Salty had a nice spot about twenty miles southwest of the town, with plenty of water—well, plenty by Arizona standards—and some rich grazing land.

For somebody who'd had an awful hard start in life, and who'd had the bad luck to be taken prisoner in the first year of the War Between the States and spend the remainder of it in a Yankee prison camp—only to be released at the war's end, then thrown into prison on a trumped-up charge just two years later—old Salty had finally fallen into quite a honey pot.

It was about time for Salty to have something go right for him, Slocum thought. It was about damn time he had a turn. Except now Salty was plagued by rustlers.

Two hundred and some head had gone missing over the last fifteen months. That was a lot of cattle to lose, a fact which Slocum shared with Hector over another fine campfire dinner. Hector could have signed on as a cook with any outfit, and set his own salary.

"Ain't nobody seen nothin' at all?" Hector asked as he poured his third cup of coffee. "Seems to me that that's a long stretch to go without somebody seeing somethin' out of the ordinary. A stranger, maybe. Or tracks. You know, a passel of cows wanderin' off the wrong way? And a horse or three wandering along right behind 'em."

Slocum nodded. "A body'd think so, wouldn't they? But nobody's seen a thing. Makes me wonder if the rustlers haven't got a man on the inside, helpin' 'em out."

"My thinkin', exactly," Hector concurred. He gestured toward Slocum with the coffeepot, and Slocum held out his cup.

"Don't know if I mentioned it," Slocum said while Hector poured him another cup, "but if Salty isn't of a mind to pay a second man, I'll split my fee with you. I'm glad to have you along."

"You did," replied Hector, "and I'm glad to be comin'. It's helpin' to take my mind off what happened to Ramona. But I'm tellin' you right now, if I get a whiff of either of those two skunks, I'm off Salty's rustlers and on those two varmints like white on rice."

Slocum took a sip of his coffee. "Hate to see you ride out, but I'd understand, Hector. I didn't tell you, but I took a walk back up to Sheriff Ploughshare's office the morning we left."

"And?"

"From what he told me," Slocum went on, "the law's bound to get hold of those sons of bitches before you do. Punk Alvarez is wanted in New Mexico for murder, plus a lot of petty stuff in Colorado and Arizona. Seems folks from Texas to California and clear up to Canada are on the scout for Lando Reese."

"But they ain't found 'em yet," Hector said softly, staring into the fire. He looked up again. "You always get a right mean expression whenever Lando's name is mentioned," he said. "He must've left a sour taste in your mouth up in Nevada. Killin' your partner and all, I mean."

Slocum nodded curtly and said, "That he did." Joey Todd, the boy Slocum had reluctantly partnered up with, had been just a kid, green and eager and fresh from New Jersey, but with a genuine talent for finding bright metal. Talent? He could practically sniff it out of the earth!

Slocum had had his doubts about Joey at first, but had grown to like the kid tremendously. He'd taken him to his first whorehouse, taught him to ride without falling off or looking like a blamed idiot, and seen him blossom into a real Westerner.

Or start to, anyway. Lando Reese had ended Joey's life before he'd reached his twenty-second birthday, ended it in the back room of the Bee Café in Bent Elbow, Nevada, by ramming a fireplace poker through his midsection. Joey hadn't had a chance, but he'd lived just long enough to describe his killer to Slocum. Slocum had recognized Lando right off.

Almost four years was a very long time to have unfinished business, and it gnawed on him.

Softly, Slocum said, "I want Lando about as bad as you do, Hector. Maybe worse."

"Like you told me about fifty times in the past few days," Hector said as he stirred the fire, "be patient, my friend."

"Thought you was comin' with a couple of boys, Lando," Tinker said. They were sitting off a ways from the other men, and it was the first chance they'd had to speak privately.

"I was," Lando replied around the pocketknife he was carefully picking his teeth with, "but one'a the bastards took a fancy to a horse what wasn't his."

Tinker snorted. "Hell, that never bothered you before."

"This time, it was about two blocks from the sheriff's office," Lando replied. He folded his pocketknife and put it away. "And somethin' about that nag bothered me. Had a bad feelin' about it, that's all. That, or mayhap the feller that owned it. I don't know. Anyway, Punk and Gordo and me, we split up."

Night had fallen, and despite the blanket of stars and the clear night, Lando could barely see his brother through the gloom. It had been almost a year since they'd been together, but Tinker hadn't changed a whit. Still full of piss and vinegar, and ready, willing, and able to take on Satan himself.

Both brothers were taller than average. About six feet even with their boots on, Lando guessed, although he'd never bothered to measure, exactly. Both had the same shade of dark reddish-brown hair, both were brown-eyed, and both, having suffered from the ravages of acne in their teens, had badly pockmarked faces. There were only two years between them, Tinker being the youngest, and they looked enough alike that Lando had been prone to say that he didn't need a mirror to shave in, he had Tinker. Well, except for that eye.

The shaving bit didn't make much sense when you studied on it close, but it seemed like a funny thing to say.

This was about as far as Lando's sense of humor went.

Tinker, with his left eye slowly roving over the scene, was talking about the cattle. "Sound good to you?" he asked.

"What?" Lando replied. Then he shrugged and added, "Sorry, Tinker. Weren't listenin'."

Tinker shook his head. "I might have me a wanderin' eye, but you got a wanderin' brain, brother. I was sayin' that Cole wants to pick up another twenty or thirty head before we push this bunch down south of the border. Day after tomorrow, I'm thinkin'. You up for it?"

Lando nodded. "Fine by me."

"Course," Tinker went on, "he was right disappointed when you come in alone. If'n we'd had more men, we could rustle more steers and drive a bigger herd south."

"I know," Lando said, a little impatiently. "Everybody keeps telling me that. Cole himself about four times. Christ!"

Lando wasn't any too wild about this Cole character Tinker was mixed up with. And that Tinker had now gotten *him* mixed up with, damn it. Not that he'd said anything discouraging to Tinker. He supposed that was the biggest difference between them. He was a natural-born leader, and Tinker? Tinker was a natural-born follower, who, for the moment, anyway, had chosen to trail after a cocky little bastard—little being the operative term, for he was barely five-foot-five in his boots—named Cole Strait.

And Cole bothered Lando. He was too damn big for his britches, that was it, what with hollering orders around and not letting anybody else have any say in things. Short men like Cole always seemed to have something to prove, Lando supposed. Cole was currently shoving his weight around by treating Lando Reese like he was a nobody. Lando Reese, who was wanted in four states and three territories!

Now, Lando figured he'd take it for a while. After all, he was new to Cole's campfire, and there was Tinker to think of. Tinker thought the sun rose and set off Cole's ass.

But if, as time went on, Cole wanted to prove something and use Lando as an example? Well, Lando figured there was a limit to charity, by God. Mr. Big Boss Cole Strait was going to find himself six feet under before he could say "boo."

That was all there was to it.

Tinker grinned at Lando about then, and his teeth, white and even, glinted in the moonlight. The Reese brothers had been blessed with nice teeth, both of them. Women were always telling Lando what pretty teeth he had.

Tinker said, "Now, don't take on so, brother. You an' me both know you're worth three men in any scrape. Cole'll figure that out soon enough."

"Yeah, sure," growled Lando, who was still mad, thinking about Cole, that pompous little shit. Just because a man had done some dirt way back in the war years didn't mean squat to him. "Stop butterin' it."

Tinker chuckled, then pulled out his fixings bag and began to roll himself a smoke. "So, what you been up to, Lando? It's been a spell."

Lando fished in his pocket and brought out the remaining two-thirds of a cigar he'd been saving. He lit it up while Tinker was still shaking out tobacco. "Not much, little brother, not much."

What he'd done to the camel, and the fact that he'd burnt down a ranch, seemed like such small things that they weren't even worth mentioning. Neither was the settler's wife he'd raped over in California or the botched bank job up in Colorado, especially since he'd let two of his own men get killed in that one.

But he said, "Killed me a few Mex bandits. Cut their peckers off and dried 'em, and strung 'em on a latigo thong."

Tinker gave his quirlie a last lick and stuck it in his mouth. "Say now! You got 'em with you?"

"In my saddlebags."

"Can I see?"

"Sure," Lando said, and stood up. "C'mon. I'll show you."

Hector, who was on watch, leaned hard against a granite boulder with his pistol in his hand. He'd drawn it with excruciating slowness, and now he cocked it just as slowly and carefully, with as little noise and movement as possible.

The cat was working its way down through the rocks and thin vegetation with equal carefulness, except that the cat's stealth was in anticipation of a nice horsemeat dinner. Hector's was for another reason entirely.

He waited until the mountain lion—which appeared to be a young one, from what he could glimpse through the weeds and brush—was just a few feet from a place just above the horses, a place Hector guessed that he'd choose to spring from. The wind was blowing toward the cat, and the horses, drowsing in their hobbles, hadn't caught a whiff of him yet.

If that cat thought he was going to make dinner out of Tico and Creole, he had another think coming.

Hector had started slowly to raise the barrel of his gun, to inch it up, when Slocum rolled over in his sleep and began to snore like a goddamn lumberjack.

Which woke up the horses, and stopped the young cat dead in its tracks. And just about gave poor Hector a heart attack.

Well, hell. He was too tired to waste the rest of the night waiting for that cat to come in the rest of the way. He brought up his pistol, took aim at the rock directly beside the crouched mountain lion's head, and fired.

Both horses reared and tried to run when the blast went off, but their hobbles didn't let them get more than a few feet.

Slocum sat straight up, twisting his head like an owl, and the mountain lion, whose hide was still faintly dappled with the last of his juvenile spots, took off in a big hurry.

Probably with a face peppered by rock chips.

"Scat, cat," Hector muttered, and holstered his gun. "Get gone, *el gato*. Go and catch yourself a rabbit or a pack rat."

"What?!" cried Slocum. It was a fair guess that he was pretty confused, what with Hector sitting there so calm and all, but to his credit Slocum was already on his feet with his Colt in his hand, and he looked more than willing to use it.

Fast son of a bitch, that Slocum.

The horses had settled down some, although they were still looking a tad white around the eyes, and Hector stood up. He said, "Sorry. Nothing. Go back to sleep."

Slocum swung that Colt of his around and aimed it straight at Hector's belly. *"Nothing?"* he growled. "You're firin' a gun off for *nothing*?"

Hector shrugged. "Scared off a cat, that's all."

Slocum's pistol barrel slowly sank toward the ground. "Jesus," he muttered in annoyance. And then, in what seemed like an afterthought, he asked, "You get it?"

"Didn't try," Hector said calmly, staring toward the horses. They needed a soothing hand. "Cougars has got to eat, same as anybody. This'un was a youngster. I just let him know he'd best look elsewhere for his supper."

"Jesus," Slocum repeated under his breath, and jammed his Colt back into its holster. He pulled his blanket back up to his chin, pulled his hat back down low, over his eyes, and muttered, "Next time, warn a fella, goddamn it."

5

Bob Chavez rode in through the pass at about ten the next morning. Lando Reese and Cole Strait stepped up to meet him as he dismounted his sweating mare. Bob was grinning from ear to ear.

"Well?" Cole demanded before the man had chance to catch his breath. "Spit it out!"

Lando, who was standing a little behind Cole, rolled his eyes. Cole had been lecturing Lando on his "rules" all morning. There was a word for men like him. Martinet, that was it. The man was a pint-sized tyrant like that little French guy, old Whatshishame. What did he think this was, anyway? The goddamn army?

If it hadn't been for Tinker's attachment to the sawed-off little shit, he would've been dead about ten minutes after breakfast.

Bob Chavez, still huffing from his ride, said, "Rolly says bring the whole herd."

"The hell I will," Cole growled.

"No, really, Boss," Bob insisted. "We found round about thirty head of Lazy D cows strayed way off west." He grinned and pointed. "They're even farther west, now, and Salty Nelson's boys ain't gonna be lookin' for

41

'em. I took a swing over that way, and now they got a little grass fire to put out." Bob smirked self-importantly. "Might'a sorta accidentally spread to their barn, too."

Cole eyed him silently, but Lando thought it was a fine idea. Just head this bunch down to meet those new cows, and they'd be on their way, slicker than snot.

Bob must have grown tired of waiting for an answer—or congratulations on his fire-setting skills—because he said, "Well, that's just what you said, ain't it? Twenty or thirty head more this time, and then we could push 'em down to Mexico?"

Cole scratched the back of his head, and Lando was thinking that old Cole had better jump on this chance, or he'd by-God add another pecker to that necklace he was stringing, when Cole said, "Rolly still down there with 'em?"

Bob shook his head energetically. "We pushed 'em into a little box canyon. You know, that one what we used before. He can hold 'em till we get there if'n we don't stand around scratchin' our asses too long."

Cole shot Bob a look that made all the color drain out of Bob's face, and he added quickly, "Or I suppose we could drive 'em back up here. If'n you wanted."

Lando was half-expecting Bob to tack a "Your Majesty" on the end of it.

Cole studied on this long enough that Lando was beginning to suspect that he didn't have a full ladle of brains, but then he turned toward Lando. "Holler your brother down from the rocks, then get saddled. We're moving the herd. Bob, you break camp."

Jesus Christ, Lando thought as he climbed up the ancient stone steps chiseled into the rock face. *What the hell does Tinker see in Cole, anyway?*

Giving himself a final heave, he at last topped the wall of the canyon and waved his hat at his brother, who was standing guard at the distant entrance to the pass. He cupped his hands around his mouth and shouted, "Come on in, Tinker! We've movin'!"

And while Lando stood there waiting as Tinker, holding his rifle wide for balance, navigated the rocky surface, he was figuring ways that maybe he could deal with Cole. Maybe the others, too.

After all, this small herd Cole had put together would bring a lot more money if it was split just two ways.

"I swear to God, Slocum, every time I figure we're just about there, you say we've gotta climb another goddamn mountain," Hector complained. "You got somethin' against the flatlands?"

Slocum hiked one corner of his mouth. Hector had been bitching since they broke camp, but Slocum didn't mind. At least it had taken Hector's mind off Ramona. Or at least he hadn't mentioned the camel all morning.

"Hector, if you're not of a mind to ride up this one, I reckon I can cut you a break," he said magnanimously. "We'll go around the son of a bitch. Happy now?"

"Hot damn," Hector said dryly.

"Appreciate your enthusiasm," Slocum replied, and reined Creole to the south. Hector followed along.

For a time both men were silent, and there was only the creak of saddle leather and the plod of hooves, the chirp and coo of birds, and the thin whine of the soft breeze cutting through the brush and rock. But just as they turned off a narrow trail that skirted the peak of a low mountain and onto a wider path, Hector's stomach growled.

"You say somethin'?" Slocum asked, straight-faced.

Hector replied, "Said we'd best stop and have somethin' to eat."

Slocum nodded. "Wouldn't mind." Noontime meals on the trail were quick and easy, but Slocum was looking forward to some of those biscuits left from breakfast and the last of the fried jackrabbit.

He pointed down the hill a ways, toward a wide flat place with a good view of the flats to the south. "Down there?" he asked.

Hector nodded. "As long as it's lower, it suits me fine."

Forty minutes later, they had watered the horses and loosened their girths, and Hector was breaking out the cold grub when Slocum caught a glimpse of something moving far to the south.

"What?" Hector asked when Slocum stood up, went to his horse, and pulled his spyglass from his saddlebag.

"Tell you in a minute." Frowning, Slocum rested his elbows on Creole's rump and raised the glass to his eye.

There were four riders, he finally decided. It took him a minute, because the riders were all mixed up with about a hundred head of cattle—and the ensuing dust cloud—and moving into the distance at a brisk trot. They were on Salty Nelson's land, all right, but they were leaving it in something of a hurry. And they were headed straight toward a long stand of rocks on the horizon.

"What the hell is it, Slocum?" Hector demanded. "You got a curious look on your face, boy."

"You're not gonna believe this," Slocum said, lowering the spyglass and collapsing it with a snap, "but I think we might just have found Salty's rustlers."

Three hours later, Slocum and Hector were down on the flat grassland, following the herd's wide and beat-down path at a jog. They were nearly halfway across the plain, and the little clump of rocks in the distance was rapidly becoming a low range of hills.

"We're gonna look real stupid if these fellas have got

them a bill of sale," Hector said for perhaps the fourth time.

Slocum didn't answer him. He figured it was better to look a little stupid than to take a chance on a hundred head of Salty Nelson's beeves disappearing down into Sonora. And he was beginning to feel a little cocky, what with the possibility of having found the rustlers right off the bat, before he so much as checked in with Salty at the Lazy D.

Now, that would be something, wouldn't it?

And besides, there were only four men up ahead with those cows. Hector was as good as any two. So was he, for that matter. He figured the odds were about even, maybe even tipped some in their favor.

"Stop smilin', goddamn it," Hector growled.

"Sorry," said Slocum. He hadn't realized he was.

"You sure there are only four?"

"Yup."

"Swear on your mama's grave?"

"Yup."

Hector sighed. "Well, I reckon you can smile a little."

"Yup," replied Slocum, and grinned. For a change, he was having some real good luck.

Rolly Clum clambered down from his perch high above the herd, which milled below him in the little box canyon. Rolly was balding and a little thick around the middle and the most solemn of the five rustlers, but he'd been around, all right. Fought Mexican *bandidos,* fought Indians and took a spear in his side, by God. Took a handful of scalps, too. He'd rousted squatters at the point of a gun, chased Chink interlopers from the California gold fields, and he'd even held up a couple of stages in his time. Well rounded, that's how he liked to think of himself.

And Rolly was smart enough to know trouble when he saw it.

"Two men," he said to Cole as he skittered down the last few feet. He collapsed his spyglass with a dull click. "Ridin' an Appy and a bay, looks like. And they're followin' our trail. I told that damn Bob we shoulda waited till tomorrow," he added in disgust. "Them clouds are moving in from the east. It woulda rained tomorrow night and covered our tracks quick, bet you anything."

Cole drew himself up, all the way to five-foot-five. "There're only two, for Christ's sake," he snapped. "You and Lando, see to it."

"Hold on." It was Lando, just riding up out of the herd.

Now, "hold on" was something you didn't say to Cole, and Rolly half-expected him to just draw his sidearm. But before things could get interesting, Lando added, "If what Rolly, here, is sayin' is the truth, I know them boys. It's Punk and Gordo."

Cole hiked an annoyed brow. "The two you were supposed to bring with you? You're sure?"

Lando blew air out between pursed lips. "Sure as I can be. At least one of 'em. Now, Punk rides a gray, but he mighta swapped it or stole a new one. But that Appy—it's a red leopard, right, Rolly?"

Rolly nodded. "Sure is."

"Well, that red leopard is the horse Gordo swiped over in Pozo Artesiano," Lando said. "It's them all right—or at least one of 'em. Can't say I'm real happy with 'em for trailin' me, though."

Cole just stood there, mulling it over. Rolly figured that someday Cole would kill him or he'd kill Cole. It was a toss-up. Unless, of course, one of these other fellers beat him to it. The only thing that had held him off, so far as he could tell, was that Cole blustered just enough to keep him knocked off balance, and paid him good enough that he was always eager for his next cut of the pie, no matter how distasteful the getting of it might be.

But someday, old Cole was gonna push somebody too hard. Unlike his baby brother, Tinker, who was still impressed enough to put up with about anything, Lando didn't seem the sort who stood for much pushing at all—a fact to which Cole was about as sensitive as the proverbial bull in a china shop.

Rolly wasn't the sharpest tool in the shed, and he knew it. He was aware that he'd fallen into the cream with Cole and his cattle schemes. Hell, hadn't he followed Cole from Texas to New Mexico and finally to here? But he knew he wasn't sharp enough to take over should some serious accident—like a knife in the ribs or a bullet to the head—befall Cole.

And he couldn't do it himself, anyway, not unless something serious happened, like Cole being caught under a rockslide with both his arms broke. Cole never seemed to sleep—the man wasn't hardly human at all, Rolly thought—and he always knew just where everybody's gun hand was. Even, it seemed, if they were in the next town.

But Lando Reese . . . Now, there was a man he figured might best old Cole. And Rolly believed Lando was a man he could follow. Still, a fellow couldn't be too sure. Lando might turn out to be as much of a peckerwood as Cole was.

Rolly sighed, then stood silently and waited for somebody to tell him what to do.

At last, Cole wiped his hand on his britches like he had something nasty on it, puckered up his dark little face, and said, "We'll start the cattle out of the canyon and moving south. Lando, you ride out and meet those men and bring 'em along."

Rolly, having received no direct orders, turned and started to walk toward his horse.

As he mounted up and rode quietly back through the herd in preparation to drive them from the canyon, he saw Lando wave to Tinker, then make a dirty gesture toward Cole's back.

Rolly turned his head and hid a snicker. The next few days were going to be interesting, all right.

Once the cattle were headed south, Cole Strait settled in riding right flank. He figured to move them another two days before he settled into the business of cutting out the newest acquisitions and changing their brands. His buyers in Mexico didn't care much about fresh and ooz-ing brands, so long as they matched the papers Cole had in his pocket.

The papers he had right now said that he was ferrying cattle from the Lightning P, and transforming the Lazy D was a piece of cake, even with that old running iron tied behind Bob's saddle.

He just wished he'd picked up a better crew. Oh, they'd pushed quite a few head to Mexico in the last year and a half, but he hadn't had a decent night's sleep in all that time. He didn't trust any of them, save maybe Tinker Reese. And he'd have to watch Tinker, too, now that his smart-aleck brother had shown up. Cole didn't trust that son of a bitch any farther than he could throw him.

Cole was tired. Tired of being in charge, although to his mind "in charge" was his natural place in the order of things. But he was tired of sleeping on the ground and tired of looking over his shoulder twenty-four hours a day.

He hadn't told the boys yet, but this was his last trip down to Mexico. Once they got these cattle sold off, he was going to head farther south, to a dusty little Mexican hamlet he knew, a town where sweet Conchita was waiting.

They'd get married, Conchita and he, and he'd settle down. Nobody in Paso Pedregoso, save Conchita, knew who he was, or who he had been. Nobody there cared that he was short, or stole cattle, or that he'd robbed banks or held up stages. Nobody cared about—or knew of—his military record.

All they knew, from his brief visits to their little hamlet, was that he was a kind man who always brought gifts, a good man who had helped them rig an irrigation system to water their crops, a brave man who had stood down—and killed most of—a gang of *bandidos* that had been plaguing them for years.

Kind, good, and brave. He liked the ring of it. He sure as hell liked it better than what he knew most of these lazy good-for-nothing bastards he was working with thought of him.

"Bob!" he suddenly shouted across the backs of the ponderously moving herd. "Bob Chavez! Wake up!"

Bob's head came up off his chest, and he reined his horse away from too-close horns, shrugging with embarrassment.

Morons, Cole thought in disgust. He'd be glad to be rid of them.

He checked his watch again. Lando should be showing up with his friends anytime now.

He glanced back, over his shoulder. He couldn't see much through the roil of dust the cattle were kicking up, though.

He put the watch back in his pocket. With two more men, they could move faster and easier, and that was good. He just hoped these two fools weren't crazy enough to expect a full cut, not for just showing up at the last minute.

He looked over at Bob Chavez again. The man's chin

was on his chest once more, and his horse was wandering out to the side. Cole reined in his mount and turned back, looking across the herd until Tinker came in sight. When he caught Tinker's attention, he gestured up toward the dozing Bob, and Tinker took off at a lope.

He watched as Tinker rode up right beside Bob and shoved him off his horse.

"Morons," he mumbled as the newly wide-awake Bob scrambled to his feet. "I'm well out of it."

6

"Company comin'," Slocum said with a scowl as he reined in his horse.

Out across the wide, grassy plain, a lone horseman had come into view. He rode toward them at a lazy lope over the brush and grass and weeds the cattle had already trampled in their passing.

"Don't seem awful upset to see us," Hector commented. With a soft creak, he leaned forward, palms on his saddle horn. "I mean, he ain't shootin' or nothin'. Mayhap he works for Salty Nelson."

Slocum said nothing, but he eased his Colt from its holster.

Just as the rider drew near enough that Slocum could almost make out his features, he stopped abruptly. He sat there for a moment, staring.

"What?" asked Hector just as two things happened simultaneously: Slocum cursed under his breath, and the rider wheeled his horse and took off at a gallop.

Slocum acted on pure instinct. Suddenly his Colt was holstered and his rifle was in his hands, the butt against his shoulder, and he was sighting down on the fleeing horseman.

"Hey!" yelped Hector.

Slocum pulled the trigger.

A split second later, the horse veered off the wide path and into the tall grass, and the man on his back sagged to one side, then toppled off. His horse raced ahead a few yards, then slowed down and stopped to graze. Slocum and Hector were halfway to the man by then.

"He's down, but he ain't dead," Slocum said grimly. "I think I just hit him in the shoulder. Watch yourself."

"Wish you'd tell me what I was watchin' myself for," Hector replied crankily. He'd pulled his revolver. "The day some damn dumb cow thief can—"

A shot rang out, and Hector's hat went flying. He hit the ground almost before it did, and Slocum was right behind him.

"You were sayin'?" Slocum asked.

"Oh, shut up," replied Hector as he grabbed his hat and rolled to cover.

Slocum did the same. Cover was sparse here, where the herd had gone through, but there were still a few isolated stands of prickly pear and jumping cholla to hide behind. Not too close, though, Slocum reminded himself. Jumping cholla was drawn to body heat—cow, man, horse, coyote, or whatever was fool enough to come close to it—and little clusters of sharp spines fairly flew from the plant and sunk themselves into that careless critter's hide.

The rider had fallen from his horse just outside the trampled path, and so was enjoying much deeper cover than he and Hector were. But Slocum had no idea where the son of a bitch was.

He looked to his right, and about fifteen yards away spotted a snatch of blue on the ground—a dusty denim-blue line that could only be Hector's legs—behind what was left of a cow-trampled prickly pear. "Hector!" he hissed. "Draw his fire!"

"You draw it!" came the reply. "Son of a bitch already shot my hat. Probably take off my head next!"

"Hector . . ."

"Aw, shit."

A moment later, Hector popped up momentarily and fired in the general direction in which the rider had tumbled to the ground. His shot was returned—in triplicate. Immediately, Slocum fired into the brush, toward the gunfire's origin, and was past gratified when he heard a cry.

"You lucky son of a bitch!" Hector burst out in disbelief. "Slocum, you beat everything."

"Yeah, I'm lucky all right," Slocum muttered, then called, toward the brush, "You, out there! Toss out your guns! We ain't aimin' to kill you!"

There was no reply.

Hector looked at Slocum and Slocum looked at Hector, and then Slocum signaled for Hector to creep forward. Slocum went sideways.

Slowly, they began to work their way around the unseen man. They had a decent idea where he was now, and Slocum had a good idea *who* he was. However, he didn't figure that now was exactly the time to share his suspicions with Hector. He wanted to wait until he had his hands on this bastard.

As hunkered as a monkey, Slocum crept slowly along the edge of the cattle's trail. The fellow back in the cover took another shot at Hector, but his aim was off. This didn't stop Hector from diving for cover again, but it gave Slocum a pretty good idea of which way their prey was crawling.

A few moments later, sweat rolling into his eyes and plastering his shirt to his back, he crawled his way back through the tall grasses and found a beaten down place, and blood. Not much, but enough to know that he was going in the right direction. He would have given a pair of new boots if he could have stood up. Of course, the man he was after probably would have made the same deal—Slocum knew he'd be a whole lot easier target that way.

His aching knees didn't know that, though.

Inch by inch, he crept forward, following the trail of bent and broken grass and brush. And the blood, of course. And then he spied a boot, just the toe of it, through the thick weeds.

"Drop it," he said, flattening himself against the ground. "Drop it, or I'll empty my gun your way. I'm bound to hit something."

This son of a bitch was likely hurt too bad to fire again, but you never could tell. He didn't fire, though, and Slocum heard the sound of something heavy thudding to the ground.

"That all?" Slocum asked.

Another thud, this one softer. Probably a pocket gun.

Slowly, Slocum got to his feet.

He'd been right. Lando Reese lay a few feet to the west and below him in the weeds, a scowl on his pockmarked face. Blood soaked his left shoulder and dribbled thinly from his right wrist.

Lando said calmly, "Long time, shithead. You hook up with another little boy yet?"

Slocum ground his teeth. "Give me a good reason not to finish you off right now, Lando."

Lando smiled. "You haven't got the sand."

"Don't push me," Slocum growled. "Get up."

"Like to oblige you, but my leg is broke."

"Good."

Slocum stepped forward, picked up the two revolvers that Lando had dropped, and tucked them in his belt. Then he took a step back and whistled for Creole. At the sound, Hector stuck his head up out of the grass, and Slocum waved him in.

"Found an old friend of yours, Hector," he called. To Lando, lying in the weeds, he said, "Hector's gonna be real happy to see you, Lando, real happy."

Lando sniffed. "Don't know nobody by that name."

"That's all right," Slocum said with a smirk. "He knows you."

"Why me?" Hector said for the second time. "I don't know why we don't just put a bullet through this peckerwood's head—or stake him out over an anthill, that'd be more like it—and go after the herd. I'm beginnin' to think you're lazy, Slocum."

"And I'm beginnin' to think you've got a flask you've been hiding," Slocum said, and gave his head a long-suffering shake. "I already explained this."

"I know, I know," said Hector, throwing his hands up in exasperation. "Don't go through it again on my account."

"Just don't kill him," Slocum repeated.

"Not makin' any promises."

"Hector . . ."

"Yeah, yeah," Hector muttered, and stepped up on his horse.

Lando Reese was already mounted and tied into the saddle. His arms were bound behind him, his wrist was bandaged, a makeshift splint had been constructed around his lower leg, the flow of blood from his shoulder had been stemmed, and there was a gag in his mouth. The expression on his face reminded Slocum of a badger poked with an awful sharp stick.

Slocum handed Lando's reins up to Hector. "Ride careful," he said. "And get Salty's boys on my trail as quick as you can."

Hector nodded. "You're crazy, you know that?"

"Been told."

With a last shake of his head, Hector said to his horse,

"Let's go, Tico, old son," muttered, "C'mon, camel killer," to his prisoner, and started north toward the Lazy D. Slocum stood there a few minutes watching the pair of horses move off into the distance, and then he mounted up.

Lando, true to form, hadn't told them squat about the herd or the rustlers, so they were no better off in that department—save that now the rustlers' numbers were decreased by one—than they had been before. There had been a fairly heated argument between Slocum and Hector, but in the end, Slocum had prevailed. Hector was to take Lando and head for Salty Nelson's place and help. Slocum would continue to trail the herd.

He would have gone back to Salty's with Hector if the sky hadn't looked funny to him. It was the wrong season for rain, but the clouds were heavy and moving in. It was a good bet that it would storm tomorrow, and the storm would erase all tracks, even those of a hundred cattle. When water came to the greedy desert, the bent became the straight and the trampled found new life.

Slocum figured that Hector could get Salty and his boys back here just from memory. Maybe a little farther. But the terrain ahead was hilly and full of box canyons and wandering trails and dead-end passes, and it was going to take somebody with his eye on the prize to get Salty the rest of the way to his cows. And the men who had stolen them.

"Let me kill him," Hector had said, eyeing Lando.

Slocum knew just how he felt. He had thought of a few worse things to do to Lando, worse than he'd let on to Hector, but this time they'd have to let the law take care of it.

Slocum reined Creole away and rode out to the east

better than a quarter mile, to a ridge paralleling the cattle's trail. He was close enough to see the path, but far enough out that he'd have a chance to hide if he saw somebody coming up from the other end. Somebody looking for Lando.

He expected somebody anytime now.

About ten miles out from Salty Nelson's place, Hector stopped to make water. It was nearly dark, and he hadn't stopped once to piss or to rest his horse since he'd left Slocum. Tico was tired, and he had apologized to him many times, and thanked him for his extra effort. He supposed that nag of Lando's was tired, too.

Sighing, he buttoned up his pants, walked around to the near side of Lando's horse, pulled the slip knot that secured the man into his saddle, and dragged a surprised Lando down to the ground.

Hopping on one foot, Lando snarled, "Gah ish," through his gag.

"Restin' the horses, you piece of shit," Hector replied.

Lando rolled his eyes. "Gah ish!" he said with more urgency. And more venom, if that were possible.

"Damn," Hector muttered and, stepping behind Lando, removed his gag.

Lando worked his mouth around for a minute before he said, "I gotta piss, you damned knothead."

"Piss, then," Hector replied curtly. "Makes me no nevermind."

"In my pants?"

Hector just stared at him for a moment, and then caved in. "All right. But you try anything, you're gonna find yourself in a pine box."

"Got a shot-up wrist and a busted leg," Lando snarled. "How the hell you figure I could try anything more than hoppin' in a circle?"

Hector worked at the ropes that bound Lando's arms behind him, then stepped back. Lando was a nasty piece of business, all right, and Hector figured not to trust him a whit. "All right," he said, resting his hand on the butt of his gun. "Piss."

Lando rubbed at his arms the best he could with that bum wrist, and said, "You don't make anything easy, do you?"

"You didn't make it easy for my Ramona, either."

"Who gives a rat's ass about a stinkin' camel, anyway?"

That did it. Hector forgot to be careful, forgot everything. He backhanded Lando as hard as he could, and Lando crumpled to the ground.

Hector didn't have any time for satisfaction, though. The moment Lando hit the ground, he hooked one boot behind Hector's knee, leveraged it with the broken leg against Hector's boot, and with an enormous cry of pain, knocked Hector down.

Surprised, Hector fell backwards and landed with a thud. His first reaction was to just shoot the son of a bitch, but when he reached for his Colt he found nothing but holster. Panting, Lando lay next to him, his face full of pain, pointing Hector's own damned gun at him.

"You sorry shit," Hector muttered.

"Not as sorry as you're gonna be," Lando said, pushing himself away through the thin grass. He dragged himself over to his horse, and pulled himself up by the stirrup until he stood, wavering, on one leg. The Colt was still pointed at Hector's heart.

"No," he said when Hector started to rise, to meet his maker standing on his feet. "Stay down, asshole."

He grabbed a handful of reins, then steadied himself on the saddle again. "All the time I've been ridin' with you, you been talkin' to that damn horse of yours.

Talked until I thought I was gonna upchuck. Seems to me a man who's as crazy about critters as you—who'd track a man for killin' a goddamn shit-heel camel, for Christ's sake!—well, the best way to hurt him is to kill another critter."

"No," Hector heard himself say. He was prepared to die if there was no way out of it, but not poor Tico, not his horse!

Before that one breathy word had left his lips, Lando fired. Tico made a terrible noise and went down, and without thinking, Hector raced to him. Left-handed, Lando had still been close enough to shoot him in the back and sever his spine, shoot him where he would take hours or days to die. The horse struggled frantically to get up. Struggled in the front, anyway. His hindquarters remained motionless.

Eyes tearing, Hector leapt over the thrashing horse, a hoof dealing a glancing blow to his arm in the process. Lando hadn't taken his rifle, which was still in its boot. Which was under Tico.

With Herculean effort, he wrenched the rifle free and swung around toward Lando. But Lando wasn't there. He was riding at a dead run back the way they had come.

Hector got off a shot, but he knew it was too far. Helplessly, he watched while Lando sped off into the distance.

Tico had stopped struggling, and lay softly groaning, his nostrils wide, his eyes ringed with white. Hector dropped to his knees at the horse's head. He was sobbing now, but he didn't care. There was no one there to see except for Tico, and he had shared tears with Tico before.

He set the rifle down and carefully lifted the horse's head to his lap. "I'm sorry, my old friend," he said, straightening Tico's forelock, wiping the dust from his beautiful face. "We've had some times together, you and I, haven't we. Ten years, we've been together. Your legs were so spindly when you were born, I thought you would never stand. But then, I've told you this before, haven't I?"

Tico quieted at the sound of his voice, and Hector just sat there for a while, telling Tico all about heaven and what good things waited for horses there.

And then slowly, he stood up and rested the tip of the barrel just above Tico's eye. *"Vaya con Dios, mi amigo,"* he whispered.

He pulled the trigger.

Slocum made a cold camp that night. In the absence of Hector's good cooking, which he greatly missed, he ate goat jerky and hardtack and washed them down with water. The clouds had closed in and stars only peeked through at intervals. Even the moon was hidden, making only a dull glow through the clouds, and it had grown so humid that the air was thick enough to cut.

Nobody had come looking for Lando, after all. On one hand, this surprised him greatly. When four fellows pushing a hundred head of beef suddenly lost a man, they'd be hurting. On the other hand, maybe Lando was such a pain-in-the-ass hard case that even those rustlers were glad to be rid of him.

Slocum sat there in darkness mulling this over and wishing for a fire and a hot cup of coffee, when he heard the distant sounds of a horse. A horse down below, on the trail, galloping full out.

He shot to his feet immediately, for what little good it did. He couldn't see that far through the gloom, couldn't even make out the broad path cut by the cattle. Whoever was riding down there was a fool, that was for certain. That horse of his would likely bust a leg in no time.

But it just kept on running, kept running until he couldn't hear it anymore; kept running south, toward the stolen cattle, toward Mexico.

7

It was a long morning's walk, that last ten miles to the ranch.

Long and hot and increasingly sultry. Lonely, too, for Hector was still deep in mourning for Tico. He'd pulled his saddle and bridle and built a pyre of dried grass and brush over the gelding, and then grimly tossed a match to it.

He'd sat nearly the whole night tending the blaze, sickened by the smell of cooking horseflesh. There was no more horrible stench, especially when it was a horse you'd known and loved. It was better than letting the coyotes feed on Tico, though.

And with every breath Hector took, that smell fed his hatred for Lando Reese, ran it through his system like a fast-growing cancer.

By late the next morning—although it was hard to tell by the sky, it was so dark and threatening—a saddened and footsore and sweated-through Hector finally limped within sight of the Lazy D. He was picked up by a lanky, redheaded, and very suspicious hand named Lenny. But once Hector explained his business, Lenny put his pistol away and dropped him on the front porch of Salty Nelson's ranch house.

"Sorry 'bout the gun," Lenny said before he reined his horse away. "Can't be too careful, lately. Got rustlers." And then, rather belatedly, he asked, "What happened to your horse?"

"Shot," Hector replied. He didn't much feel like going into detail. He stared out over the still-smoldering remains of Salty Nelson's barn and asked, "Your rustlers did that?"

"Couldn't be no other," Lenny shouted grimly from halfway across the yard. "Got the boys out lookin' to see what mischief they was tryin' to call our attention away from."

"I think I know what that was," Hector muttered. He rapped on the door.

It was answered immediately by a gruff-looking man, about five-foot-ten, grizzled of hair and lean of frame, with a very large and very black handlebar mustache. Hector blinked.

"Well?" barked the man, who was hatless and wiping his hands on what looked like a tea towel. Hector also realized, with a start, that the man had false teeth, and not very good ones, either. After that one-word greeting, the man stuck his thumb in his mouth, pad-side up, and pushed the top choppers back into place.

"You Salty Nelson?" Hector asked.

Eyeing him, the man nodded curtly.

"Slocum sent me."

Salty Nelson's scowl suddenly bloomed into a wide grin. "By God!" he said, and gave his uppers a little adjustment again. " 'Bout damn time!"

And with that, he reached out, took hold of Hector's shoulder, and pulled him straight into the house.

The sky was far too gloomy for midday, Slocum thought as he dogged the cattle's trail. The skies would open in an hour or two, if he was any judge. Already he could see lightning flashing through the black clouds to the west and south. He'd been watching it almost the whole of the morning, but it was rapidly growing closer. The dry booms of thunder that had seemed distant earlier in the day were now loud enough that sometimes they practically knocked him from the saddle.

Like his daddy used to say, it was going to be a real goose-drownder.

He hoped that Salty Nelson's boys had got an early start. If they had, and if they were traveling fast, they might reach him within the next two hours. It couldn't be soon enough to suit his taste.

The herd had moved south, out of the grasslands and into the range of hills known less than affectionately as No Man's Land. It was easy to get yourself permanently lost in its maze of dead ends and tight box canyons and waterless valleys. Easy, too, to drown in a low spot or a pocket when the rains came unexpectedly.

He figured that his safest bet, when the skies opened, was to just get up high and hope for the best.

And he was still bothered by that horseman who had galloped past him last night, hell bent for leather. What kind of fool tried for that kind of speed in that black a night?

There were several explanations, of course. Somebody might have been sending for a doctor. Of course, he didn't know of any towns down this way, but then, he hadn't been down this way for a few years.

It might have been a courier, heading lickety-split from Tucson to the next military post to the south—or more likely to the next remount station, where he could pick up a fresh horse to replace the one he was running into the ground. A message that couldn't be telegraphed for one reason or another.

But he didn't figure either of those—or any of the other explanations he'd come up with—held water. All he knew was that he had a real bad feeling about it.

Thunder boomed, so close that Creole skittered to the left. Slocum took hold of him immediately, gathering his reins and cursing under his breath. But Creole, who had been stepping carefully along the edge of a sharp, uneven rise, slipped and skidded sideways.

Creole was as athletic as a cat, but even cats have bad days. Being unable to get any traction on the gravelly surface of the hillside, he slid, spinning and scrambling and finally tumbling down the slope to the bottom. Slocum was thrown clear, landing sharply on his hip, and Creole landed on his back.

Slocum was on his feet immediately and raced, as well as he could, toward the horse. Creole climbed to his feet with a shudder and a shake just as Slocum realized there was something wrong with his hip, really wrong. He nearly went down, and fell against the horse, grabbing the dangling reins to catch his balance.

Creole, who wasn't exactly happy about having come down the hill ass-over-teakettle and then having his head jerked around, threw his noggin up and back against that sharp grab of the reins, and Slocum was nearly lifted off his feet.

"Ho, dammit!" he shouted.

Creole eyed him, his nostrils wide. But he held still.

"Sorry," Slocum said gruffly. "Sorry." His hip hurt like a bastard, but when he grabbed hold of the saddle and tried to move his leg, it moved. It wasn't broken, but pain shot through him like a knife. He supposed that if it had been busted, he never would have made it to Creole in the first place.

"All right," he muttered through clenched teeth, "Let's see about you."

He clucked to the horse and moved him in a little circle around his body, taking care to move himself as little as possible. The horse seemed sound enough, if shaken.

Slocum rubbed the gelding's neck. "It's all right, fella. Good boy. That damn thunder woulda scared anybody. Now, if I can just get back up into the saddle . . ."

After four attempts he finally managed it, and nearly bit a hole in his own cheek from trying, out of nothing more than habit, to stifle his cries of pain. Whatever was pulled or busted in there wasn't a bone, but it was surely something major. Eyes tearing in spite of himself, he sat quietly atop Creole, trying to figure out what came next.

And as he sat there, a big, fat drop of warm rain landed on his hand. And then another. And another. And suddenly, the heavens just opened and all the water in the world was coming down in sheets, in rivers.

"Son of a goddamn *bitch*!" he muttered. The water was already up to Creole's fetlocks, and gushed from Slocum's hat brim. And naturally, Slocum's waterproof duster was just where he'd left it—tied behind his saddle.

Trying his best to ignore the pain, he reined Creole ahead, to a gentler rise. There would be no shelter. Nothing grew in No Man's Land. He and Creole would just have to wait it out.

Bad luck, real bad luck. But he figured he was having good luck on one count. The men up ahead were pushing a sizable number of cattle—the hundred head, or thereabouts, that they'd started out with, and the twenty-five or thirty that they'd picked up several miles later. There were only three men left that he was aware of, and storms spooked cattle.

Additionally, he figured the rustlers would have a hard time of it to find any single place high enough—and relatively dry enough—to park those steers for the duration of the storm. If the herd wasn't already scattered all over hell-and-gone, that was.

As the lightning flashed overhead and the rain coursed down, he reined Creole to a halt about halfway up a rocky hill and carefully dismounted. He pulled his duster down, gave it a shake, and put it on over his soaked clothing, then limped a few feet through the mire, leading the horse. He eased himself down on a wet boulder and shifted position until he found the one that caused him the least pain.

"Son of a bitch," he repeated over the incessant beat of the rain and the ominous rolls of thunder.

Lando wasn't doing so well, either.

Tucked in the poor shelter of a large rock, splinted and aching leg stuck out before him, he watched while Tinker and the others tried in vain to hold the herd together.

He had given up on it. If Cole thought they were going to bunch these spooky beeves in the middle of a goddamn deluge, he had another think coming. They'd already lost about thirty, maybe forty head, and more were disappearing into the curtain of rain all the time.

They had stopped—more like, the rain had stopped them—in a middling-high valley. The water was draining to somewhere, that was for sure, but the cows were nervous as hell, scrambling up and over hills, scrambling out the shallow dips between them.

This goddamn valley was about as secure as a kitchen strainer.

There were about nine places where a cow could make a break for it, and only five riders to hold them back. Four, now that Lando had decided to call it quits. And he could only see one of the escape routes through the pelt, it had gotten so bad.

While he watched, two more sodden beeves made a bid for freedom. There was nobody there to stop them. He sure as hell wasn't going to try.

A horse appeared through the cascading wall of water. Lando watched while Tinker dismounted and led his horse the seven or eight feet to Lando's rock. Tinker squatted down. Over the dull roar of the pounding rain, he said, "I quit."

Lando nodded. "Cole's crazy."

Immediately, Tinker said, "Now, Lando . . ."

"Well, what do you call an idiot who wouldn't even send anybody back to check on Slocum?" Lando roared. "That fool's back there doggin' us, and this bigger fool?" he said, pointing blindly into the rain, which had taken a sudden turn for the worse. "He won't even take the time to go finish him off. What the hell's wrong with him anyways?"

Tinker didn't have any answer for that, other than "Cole knows what he's doin', I reckon." It came out pretty damn lame, though.

Which was just the opening Lando was looking for. He said, "Tinker, why don't you and me just take this herd? Once we take care of Slocum, I mean. The two of us could push 'em down to Mexico. Be hard, but we could do it."

Tinker looked at him like he'd gone loco. "A hundred and thirty steers? You crazy?"

"Gonna be more like seventy by the time we come outta this storm," Lando said grimly.

The rain let up for maybe three seconds, and Lando caught a glimpse of Bob Chavez. He'd called it quits, too, and was off his horse and huddled next to a rock maybe fifty feet away. Lando didn't have time to check the whereabouts of the others, because the skies all of a sudden started pouring barrels again, and once more, his visibility was reduced to a few feet.

"I figure the strays we don't catch'll keep this Nelson character busy till we're too far away to bother with," he went on.

Tinker shook his head. "I won't cross Cole, Lando. I know you're my brother, but I won't cross him, not even for you."

Lando took a deep breath and fought back the urge to just pound some sense into Tinker. "Why the hell not? Blood's blood, little brother, and the rest? It don't matter a damn. Say we only get seventy, seventy-five head down to Mexico. Cole's gonna take his cut, and the other four of us are gonna split what's left over. Why, you'll be lucky if you can even buy a couple'a *cervezas* with your share!"

Thunder boomed, nearly tore the skies open, and both brothers craned their heads up into the downpour.

"Big son of a bitch," said Tinker.

"She's right on top of us," said Lando.

"How's your wrist?"

"Been better," Lando grumbled.

Hector, Salty Nelson, and the men of the Lazy D—or what of them could be rounded up on short notice— were stopped a little south of the place where Hector and Slocum had split up the day before.

They had made good enough time up until now. But Hector's instincts told him they should wait for a respite in the weather, wait until they made a less intriguing target for the lightning that flashed all around them, and that had already struck a nearby outcrop of rock. Salty Nelson, however, was opposed.

"I say we go on," he was shouting over the rain. He paused to stick his thumb in his mouth and give his uppers a nudge. "Ain't no shelter out here, nohow."

Hector pointed his finger upward, toward the dark, lightning-shot sky. The sun had seemingly retired for the duration. "We're gonna get sizzled, Salty! Gonna get fried!"

"Don't give a damn!" Salty shouted back at him.

Judging by his face, he truly didn't. "Some progress is better than none, by God."

"Aw, the hell with it," Hector muttered, and urged the sorrel Salty had lent him forward, through the mire.

He might as well get killed by lightning, he thought. After all, he'd lost Lando Reese, and in doing so, had effectively killed his Tico. Everything was going wrong. Why not add a bolt of lightning to the mix? Seemed sort of circular, somehow.

He'd tried blaming it on Slocum for a little while. If Slocum had just let him kill Lando on the spot, or if they'd even hauled the bastard along with them, things would have been different. They might not have been any better, but they sure couldn't have been any worse, could they?

But in the end, he could fault no one but himself. He'd let Lando make him mad, and that had done it. Just a second of unguarded anger, and wham, Lando had gained the upper hand. Stupid. His temper was always his downfall, wasn't it?

Another horse jogged up beside him in the sheeting rain. The rider was even with him before he made out the face.

"How far?" Connie Nelson shouted.

It had been a real start, finding a woman in Salty Nelson's house, but there she'd been. She was maybe twenty-five, with dark hair and dark eyes, and Salty had said that she was his niece. He'd said it with a little shudder and an eye roll, too, as if that gal was running him ragged.

Hector hadn't seen how a pretty woman like that could make a tough old bird like Nelson nervous. Leastwise, not until they'd started mounting up and she turned up smack dab in their midst, already changed out of her dress and into a pair of denim trousers and a light blue man's shirt, with a big old Colt strapped to her hip and an "I mean business" look in her eye.

"You're not going, Connie," Salty had said about four times.

"Oh, hush, Uncle Salty," she'd replied matter-of-factly. Also four times.

She went.

And now she was riding through this downpour, soaked to the skin and chipper as a goddamn bird.

Salty wasn't pleased, Hector wasn't pleased, and Slocum sure as hell wasn't going to be pleased. The hands just looked resigned to her presence.

She pointed ahead, to where the beginning of No Man's Land would have been if they could have seen it through the storm. "Up there? To the edge?"

"No farther," he shouted.

"What then?"

"We wait for a signal from Slocum."

She nodded, as if this answer passed muster with her, then kneed her mount and moved up ahead and out of sight, probably to ride beside Salty Nelson. When Hector had first met her, he couldn't for the life if him figure out why a gal who looked like that wasn't married.

Now he knew. Bossy and headstrong, that was one reason.

And if he'd had a chance to talk to her for more than five minutes out of the whole of the time he'd known she existed, he probably could have come up with a few more.

8

The rain stopped just before dusk, and within an hour the clouds that had blanketed the skies had tattered away to nothing. The storm had spent itself, and when night came, it came clean and clear.

The rain also left a heavy chill in the air, and Slocum found himself shivering beneath his duster. He deliberated long and hard before he finally built a fire on the north side of the hill. Hopefully, it was low enough down the slope and small enough that the rustlers, far to the south, wouldn't spy it. And just big enough and high up enough that Salty Nelson and Hector, coming from the north, would.

In the meantime, he tried to dry his gear next to its feeble, smoky warmth. His boots came off, his socks were rigged on sticks next to the flame, and his boots went back on next to bare skin. His shirt and britches and smallclothes joined his socks at the fireside, and he wrapped himself back up in his duster while the coffee boiled and he cooked his supper of skillet biscuits and dried beef.

The fire was still smoking badly, even by the time he finished eating. Every twig and stick of kindling had been soaked through by the rain, and it had been a bitch to find the few sticks dry enough to get it started in the first place. He was just about to give up, to pull on his still-damp clothes, and kick out the son-of-a-bitching thing when a distant voice called, "Hello, the camp!"

Hector's voice.

He had called back, "Ride in!" before he remembered that he was stark naked underneath his duster. With the sound of crunching hooves drawing closer, he yanked off his boots again. He grabbed his smallclothes and pulled them on, then grabbed his britches and tried to pull them on, too. It was no small feat, since his hip was still hurting something fierce, and damp cloth, he soon learned, didn't exactly slide smoothly over damp cloth.

He must have taken longer than he thought, because the next thing he knew, a female voice purred, "Why, you didn't tell me there was going to be floor show, Uncle Salty."

Which comment was followed immediately by Salty Nelson's voice. "Connie! Turn your head, dammit!"

Belatedly, Slocum buttoned up his britches just in time to see the girl say, "Oh, pish!" She leaned forward on her saddle horn and smiled at him in a way that was far too knowing. "The one and only Slocum, I presume?"

Despite himself, Slocum felt color rising up to heat his neck. "Slocum, anyway," he muttered as he yanked his shirt from its makeshift prop beside the fire and shrugged into it. He looked up again. "Salty," he said curtly and with a quick nod. Salty and the girl had been joined at the edge of the firelight by three other riders, as well as Hector.

Hector thumbed back his hat, grinning.

Slocum looked at him and said, "Oh, shut up, Hector."

"Didn't say a word," Hector said innocently.

"Well, don't," Slocum grumbled. He tucked in his shirttails.

"Now, boys," the girl said, dismounting. "Let's not scrap."

"My niece, Connie," Salty said as he swung down off his mount. "I apologize in advance for everything she's gonna do to piss you off. It's good to see you again, Slocum."

The men stepped down from their saddles, too, and one of them gathered the horses and led them down the slope, to where Creole was tethered.

"Good to see you, Salty," Slocum replied. "And your little surprise, too," he added, looking the girl up and down.

She was about five-foot-five, with dark brown hair and coffee-colored eyes, and a pretty, mischievous face that had him thinking immediately of leprechauns and fairies—and wondering whether leprechauns and fairies liked to get naked with soaked-through saddle tramps. Full breasts strained the fabric and buttons of her shirt, which nipped into a tiny waist before her figure flared out again into full hips. Her legs went on forever.

"Surprise?" Salty snorted. "Nice name for her. Pain in the ass is more like it."

"Language, Uncle Salty," Connie said, although she didn't look as if his language bothered her at all. She was, in fact, looking at Slocum, eyeing him up and down the same as he was doing to her. Slocum hovered between admiration for her boldness and wanting to duck behind one of the horses, just to get away from her predatory gaze. Men were supposed to look at women like that, not the other way around!

"Man, I could about lay down in that fire," said one of the hands. Redheaded and lanky, he was hovering at its edge, and his teeth were chattering. He shot a hand out toward Slocum. "Name's Lenny, Mr. Slocum. Lenny Walsh. Right pleased to meet you."

Slocum shook his cold hand, saying, "Lenny. And it's just Slocum."

Lenny went back to leaning over the fire. "We heared what you done up in Phoenix last year. About them bank robbers and everything, I mean. That was sure some deal, if you don't mind my sayin' so. Speakin' for myself, I'm real glad you're on our side in this thing."

Salty Nelson squatted down on the other side of the smoking fire. "Quit puffin' him up, Lenny," he said gruffly. "Don't wanna have to pay him any more than I already am."

Slocum's mouth quirked up in a grin. "You ain't paid me a red cent yet, Salty. You always were a cheap old buzzard."

Another hand, crouched beside Lenny and trying his damnedest to dry out his shirt, muttered, "Ain't that the truth!"

"Aw, shut up, Orville, and get that dry firewood we brung," Lenny carped. "This wet stuff is smokin' to beat the band." Then he tipped his head toward Connie. "Her idea. Got it wrapped in a tarp."

While Orville got up from the fire and walked off, grumbling, into the darkness, Slocum said, "It was a good one."

Connie shrugged. She was still standing right where she'd landed when she dismounted, staring at him with her open duster billowing out behind her in the cold breeze and her arms crossed over her ample chest. Which he also noticed was cold. Her nipples stood out like pebbles beneath her shirt.

And she was smiling at him, goddamn it.

She said, "One has to think of the details."

Salty Nelson snorted.

"Excuse you, Uncle Salty," she said without looking

at him. She only had eyes for Slocum, and it fair to gave him the collywobbles. He felt like she was taking the clothes right back off of him, which, under other circumstances, wouldn't have necessarily been a bad thing. He did the same to women all the time, he supposed. But out here, right in front of her uncle, not to mention God and everybody else?

"So, Slocum," she said, pulling off her gloves. "Where do those thieving bastards have our cows?"

Tinker wouldn't listen no matter what Lando tried. Lando knew he wouldn't go running to Cole, blabbing what they'd discussed, but the whole thing bothered him none-the-less.

Just where did Tinker get off, thinking somebody knew better than his big brother?

He rode through the darkness, Bob off his left side as they searched for strays in the starlight. He was chilled to the bone and about everything hurt, but he couldn't stop thinking about Tinker.

Damn him, anyway!

And damn that Cole. What was so important about that sawed-off little shit? What was important enough that Tinker wouldn't cross him?

"Down there," Bob said, and Lando reined his horse to follow after Bob's. There were three steers bunched tight in a little draw, so narrow that they bumped their butts on the sides of it and deep enough that they were standing in water over their knees.

God never made a critter dumber than a cow, Lando thought, *unless it was a sheep. Or a stinking camel.*

"Gonna have to pull 'em out," Bob Chavez said, readying his lariat.

"Whatever," Lando grumbled.

Bob roped the first one. It was a clean snare, right around the steer's horns, and he pulled him up, bawling and complaining. He freed his rope and went in for the second steer.

Lando watched, leaning on his saddle horn, and the little gears in his head were going click-click-click. When Bob hauled the second one out and went in for the third, a slow smile crawled over Lando's face.

If Tinker was so dead set against getting rid of Cole, well, he could still narrow down the odds—and up his cut of the pie—couldn't he? Four ways was better then five.

Bob backed up his chestnut, dragging the reluctant steer up the little incline, and Lando nudged his mount closer.

"Hey, watch it!" Bob grumbled when Lando got too close. Bob leaned over to snake his rope free.

And when he did, Lando raised up the butt of his gun and brought it down, left-handed but just as hard as he could, over the base of Bob's skull.

He sat his horse for a while, staring at the still form, bluish in the moonlight. And then he slowly dismounted, taking care not to jar his leg, and tugged and pushed the body back into the little pocket Bob had just pulled the steers out of.

Bob disappeared beneath the water. Tiny pearls of bubble rose up for a while, then stopped altogether. The water was still again.

"Guess you're all the way dead now," Lando muttered as he climbed back on his horse.

While Lenny poured steaming coffee into Salty's tin mug, Slocum finished drawing a map in the mud with a stick.

"We're here," he said, pointing. "Now, I ain't been down this way for several years, but as I recollect, there's a canyon big enough for those steers right about here."

He dragged the stick through a series of corkscrew turns in the map to show the trail they'd have to take, then stopped it. "Right here. It ain't big, and it ain't secure, but it's the best place they'd find for holdin' those beeves through the storm. If they're smart, that's where they'd hole up. And anybody who's led you boys around by the nose for better than a year is bound to have some brains."

Salty Nelson nodded. "You figure we should get after 'em tonight?"

Hector said, "Nope."

Slocum concurred. "They're gonna be busy roundin' up strays. Be my guess that they've lost a few. And what with 'em all scattered . . ."

"Let's go, then," said Connie, and Slocum's head jerked up. He'd been so intent on drawing the map that he'd forgotten she was there. Well, almost.

He hoisted a questioning brow.

Connie huffed out a long-suffering sigh. "If they're all out chasing down strays, what's to keep us from riding in there and taking the herd back? Sure, I know we'll lose a few head, but—"

"No," barked Salty, and he said it with such force that he nearly lost his teeth. After a little fumbling with them, he said, "I wanna see every last man of them sonsabitches hang. Don't nobody come stealin' my cattle and get away with it."

"Not for more than a year or two," Hector quipped dryly.

Salty shot Slocum a look. "Either you shut that wiseacre up or I will," he grumbled.

"You'll have to excuse Uncle Salty," Connie said, scowling sweetly. "His hemorrhoids have been acting up these last few weeks."

A couple of the hands chuckled, and Salty turned bright pink and snapped, "Connie, I swear to God!"

She threw her hands up in the air. "Fine. It was just a suggestion."

Behind his hand, Slocum sucked back a grin while she retreated to her bedroll, then said, "All right then. We go in at dawn, Salty."

Salty Nelson stood up and gave his head a curt nod, muttering, "Somebody listens to me, anyway."

"You're the boss," Slocum said.

Cole and Tinker had managed to find six wayward beeves, and were slowly nudging them back to the shallow canyon where Rolly Clum was waiting, watching over the bulk of the herd.

These six had got themselves a good way out, and the two men traveled slowly over the mired ground, talking softly to each other and the weary cattle. Right at the moment, Tinker was singing "Lorena" to them. The song served to keep them from bolting off, while the horses kept slowly pushing them on.

Tinker had a real nice voice, Cole thought. Not a voice that could sing opera or anything, just a plain, nice voice. Real clear. He liked it, and the steers liked it.

He thought pretty highly of Tinker Reese, too, not that he'd mention it. But Tinker knew. When you came right down to it, Tinker was sort of like a son to him. Not like Bob and Rolly. They were just hired help and dirt-dumb to boot. But Tinker was something more. He listened, for one thing. Cole liked a man that paid attention to him for reasons other that being scared spitless.

He'd hate to cut Tinker free once they made it down to Mexico. He'd miss him, miss the singing, miss the way Tinker hung on his every word.

Well, it had to come. Maybe he'd give Tinker a little something extra out of the cattle money. Enough to get him away from that skunk of a brother and out on his own.

Maybe Lando could have a little accident after they got to Mexico.

Cole didn't much care for Lando. No, that was an understatement. He didn't trust him as far as he could throw a chuck wagon. He just plain didn't like him, that was all there was to it. It beat him how a pretty nice kid like Tinker could have a brother like that. Spooky, the way they looked so much alike.

But Cole had himself to think of. And Paso Pedregoso. And Conchita.

Tinker swung into "I Left My Darlin' in Wichita," and Cole's thoughts turned toward the man that was dogging their trail, Slocum. He knew that it had ticked off Lando something fierce when he didn't send anybody back to get rid of him. And he'd resisted sending anybody back for just that reason. It pleased him to piss Lando off.

But additionally—and more importantly—he couldn't risk lowering the number of drovers any more than he already had. Lando was supposed to show up with himself and two others and had failed, bringing only his own sorry carcass, and now it was a stove-up sorry carcass at that. Cole had been counting on those other men. They'd barely make it through No Man's Land with the five riders they had.

And to be honest, he figured that they'd just lose this Slocum character, what with the rain and all.

Cole was pretty sure he knew this maze of hills and valleys and canyons better than any man alive. And now that the rain had wiped out their tracks, they'd be able to wind and twist their way through No Man's Land with relative ease—well, as easy as they could with only five riders—unencumbered by any fools who tried to follow.

"I think it's the next hill," Tinker said softly.

"Yup," Cole replied. One more rise, and they'd turn

these steers over to Rolly. They could have a good hot cup of Arbuckle's, then head out again. They had about thirty or thirty-five head to pick up, not counting whatever Bob and Lando had brought in.

He scowled. Just thinking about Lando made him mad. If there was one thing Cole couldn't stand, it was a stupid man. He'd put up with mean and he'd put up with ornery, but stupid was really pushing it. And what Lando had done back there, riding out lickety-split to meet his "friends," then getting himself hog-tied, and then adding insult to injury by shooting that fellow's horse? Why hadn't he just shot the damn guy when he had a chance? Lando took the goddamn cake, that's what he did.

Stupid. Just plain stupid.

9

"What'd you do to your hip?"

Everybody was close to settled in for the night except Slocum, who was standing guard, and Connie, who had just crept up beside him at the top of the hill.

"Horse took a tumble," Slocum replied as he stared out over the southern horizon. It was good and dark out there. If Lando and his buddies had built a fire, they'd built it low and small and out of sight, the same way he'd built his.

"Must smart, the way you're gimping around," Connie said, and sat down like she intended to stay. She dug around in a pocket and produced a small box, opened it, and held it toward him. "Ready-made?"

Slocum hiked a brow, but took a cigarette from the box. He didn't often get store-boughts.

She stuck one between her lips, too, then poked around in search of a lucifer. Slocum beat her to it. "Here," he said, thumbnailing the head. It burst into flame, and he lit hers, then his, careful to shelter the tiny flame so that it couldn't be seen from the southern side. You never knew when some wise-ass was going to be looking for lights in the darkness.

As he shook out the sulphur tip, she blew out a plume of smoke.

"Shocked?" she said, her eyes playful.

"Should I be?"

She cocked a brow. "You're a funny sort of man, Slocum."

He took a drag. "Why? Because I ain't up in arms over the sight of a female smokin' and wearin' pants and tryin' to tell everybody what to do?"

She didn't say anything, just smiled. Lord, she was a beauty, but more than that—she fairly oozed raw, animal sex. He wondered if she knew just how lucky she was that Salty—a tough old buzzard that everybody in his right mind was afraid of—was her uncle. He'd seen the way the men looked at her.

If she hadn't been the boss's niece, she would have found herself raped six ways from Sunday, acting and looking like that.

He felt himself growing hard despite the pain in his hip, which right up until the minute she sat down had occupied his thoughts entirely. He wasn't thinking about it so much anymore.

He said, "You'd best be careful."

She arched a brow, still grinning. "About what? Being the only filly in a corral full of randy stud horses?"

Well, she'd read his mind. He sure hoped she wasn't reading his body, because he was in no shape to keep any promises that big bulge in his britches was making.

"I do just fine, Slocum," she said, blowing out a thin jet of smoke. "Don't you worry about me. I spent three years in a house in Kansas City before I found my long lost Uncle Salty. Anybody who wants something I'm not prepared to give? That son of a bitch will find himself gelded before he can say Merry Christmas."

She looked like she could do it, too. Also, like she'd done it more than once already.

"Yes, ma'am," he said, all serious. "I'll remember that."

"Course, when I find a fellow I like," she said, her voice dropping to a purr as she drew closer, "I throw away my gelding knife."

He said, "Nice of you."

"Just wanted to share," she whispered, and before he knew it, she was kissing him soft and slow.

He kissed her back, couldn't help it, and took her in his arms as she opened her mouth to him. As they kissed, leisurely, tongues doing a slow dance, he felt her slide her hand down to cover his crotch and massage him through the denim of his britches.

And then suddenly, she pulled away. She licked at her lips and, smiling, said, "You're every inch the man I hoped you'd be, Slocum."

She stood up, leaving him sitting there with a pecker so stiff he thought his britches were going to burst. Her grin widened, and she said, "Night, now."

If the circumstances had been different, if her uncle hadn't been snoring twenty feet away and if his hip hadn't been hurting like a bastard, he would have grabbed her and somehow convinced her to stay. Actually, he didn't figure she take much convincing at all. But Salty was down the slope and Slocum's hip was killing him, so he let her walk away while the taste of her was still on his lips, on his tongue.

His cock was still pounding when she reached her bedroll and settled in for the night. He looked at her as she pulled up the blankets, then looked down at that familiar swelling and muttered, "Oh, shut up."

That little prick, Cole, rode up beside Lando when he finally pushed the three steers in with the others. On his own, in the dark, bringing them in had been a good deal harder than he'd thought.

"Where's Bob?" Cole demanded, his words accompanied by vapor.

Lando fought the urge to backhand him. Instead, he said, rather noncommittally, "Be comin' in shortly, I reckon. He swung out to the south, lookin' for more strays. Get up there, cow!" He swung his coiled rope at the butt end of a laggard beast. Just a cowboy doing his job, that was him.

"Goddamn it," growled Cole, just loud enough that Lando barely made it out. Then, louder, he said, "I told you boys to stay together out there."

Lando shrugged. "Bob's idea, not mine."

Cole reined his horse away without any comment other than a scowl.

"Picky little shit, ain't you?" Lando muttered.

He reined his horse back up toward the outcrop that had given him middling shelter during the storm, and slowly dismounted. He favored his broken leg, easing it to the ground. He'd be glad when they got down to Mexico. He'd put that leg up on a pillow for a few weeks and suck down the mescal and *cerveza,* and have his fill of enchiladas and frijoles. He might just have him a few señoritas to go with it, too.

And after his leg got healed up good, after the rest of him stopped hurting, he'd come back up here. He'd find that son of a bitch, Slocum, and he'd settle his hash, by God. Maybe that stinking Hector, too. Now that he'd had time to think about it, he knew shooting Hector's horse hadn't been enough, not by a long shot.

The look on old Hector's face when that plug of his went down was pretty good, though.

Smiling to himself, he slowly sat himself down, carefully stretched his leg out before him, and drew out his fixings pouch with his good hand. Cole couldn't expect him to go out again until Bob came back, could he? After all, he'd said not to split up. And it was surely going to be an awful long time before they heard from Bob again.

Despite constantly thudding pain, he smiled.

That same night, Punk Alvarez sat in a cantina on the outskirts of Tombstone, nursing a beer. Beer was all he could afford, because he'd spent all his money on whores and hard liquor and a big steak dinner at the fanciest restaurant in town. That had been yesterday, right at the first, and he'd nearly plugged the waiter when he brought the bill. A man forgot how much things cost in one of these upstart mining towns.

Right now, he couldn't even afford a place to stay. He had just enough for two more beers, and then he was flat-as-a-pancake broke.

At the moment, this situation wasn't bothering him as much as it should have. He'd even forgotten that Lando had ridden off without him, left him high and dry in Pozo Artesiano, and all because that goddamn knuck-lehead, Gordo, had taken it upon himself to steal a nag off the rail.

He'd forgotten these things because of Mary Jane Crabtree, who was presently singing on the stage. Well, that and the whiskey he'd had earlier, before his purse got drier than Yuma sand. Mary Jane was up there in the shine of the gaslights, singing "Slew Foot Sally" in practically nothing but her underwear, and singing it just to him. She had a fine voice and a finer figure, and she had near to mesmerized old Punk.

He was in love.

Of course, he fell in love with great regularity. You'd think it was a crime, what with the names that Lando and Gordo called him. He'd taken a shine to that god-damn camel they ran across a couple of weeks ago—not that kind of a shine, no sir, but he sort of liked it.

And Lando, out of sheer persnicketiness, had tied the beast up to a rail and started shooting.

"That's all women are, you idiot," he'd said while he was reloading his gun and the critter was bleeding and fighting its rope, trying to get away. "You use 'em, then forget 'em. They're the same as livestock, and what do we do to livestock?"

Lando had emptied his gun again, just to make the point, and a point that Punk already knew, at that. And that idiot Gordo had helped him.

Punk had fired a shot into the critter's head, just to put it out of its misery. He hadn't been so mad about the camel as he had been that now he was going to have to pick up Lord knew how many spent cartridges and melt lead half the night.

Goddamn waste, if you asked him.

And now he found that his thoughts had traveled away from the lovely Mary Jane Crabtree and right back to Lando and Gordo again. Damn it, anyhow! Why, she'd finished her number and walked right off stage—gone clear back to her dressing room—and he hadn't even noticed!

Punk stood up, all five-foot-seven of him, and elbowed his way through the smoke and the noise and the crowd, toward the back-room door.

He got elbowed in the belly a few times, but he didn't complain. People were always elbowing him in the belly in crowded rooms, probably because his belly stuck out so much. It was just one of those things a fellow learned to take in stride.

He finally reached his goal and opened the door. To his right was the stage with its glowing footlights, where some jackass actor dressed in a velvet suit was reciting from a play. Straight ahead was a dark hallway.

Punk wove unsteadily down the hall, passing the fanning light that spilled from beneath doors and squinting at the makeshift signs that hung on every one.

He went past "Sloan Acrobats" and "Tichnor's Amazing Dogs" and "Lana and Her Lovely Ladies" and at last came to the right door. There was a crudely made sign that said "Miss Crabtree" and a crookedy gold star on it.

He knocked before he remembered to take off his hat.

"What?" a female voice barked from inside.

Punk opened the door.

Miss Mary Jane Crabtree sat before a big mirror, surrounded by tables and shelves filled with sparkly glass figurines, and she was pulling off her eyelashes.

For a moment, this gave Punk a start. He'd never seen anybody take off their eyelashes before, and it took a second for it to settle in on him that she still had some of her own lashes left on her face, and that the ones she was pulling off were fake.

She cocked a brow, and said, "Well? You must be new. Did Jess see to those lights like he promised?"

"It's me," Punk said.

"Beg pardon?" She slung an arm over the back of her chair and turned to face him, and a look of understanding came over her features. "Oh. One of my admirers, I take it?"

Punk nodded. She had smeared some kind of cream over half her face, but he barely noticed, being riveted by the sight of her breasts pushing from beneath that robe of hers, which had rucked to one side when she turned. He was pretty sure she was naked as a jaybird under there, and equally certain that at any moment, the little pink center of her booby was going to poke right out from behind that old robe. Rosebuds, his daddy used to call them.

"I got money," he said. He didn't figure he needed to tell her how much—how little, actually—he had on him, just that he was a man of means. It looked like she'd been waiting just for him.

"So do I," she replied. "So what?"

"I'll pay," he offered. "I love you. Won't take me long."

She sighed, and with that breath, her nipple slipped free. While he stared at it, she said, "All right, cowboy, I get your drift. But you're in the wrong place for that. I can't figure why every Tom, Dick, and Harry thinks that just because a girl's on the stage, she's fair game for—"

Suddenly, Punk pulled her straight out of that chair and fairly tossed her on the ratty fainting couch. Half the figurines went crashing to the floor.

"I said it wouldn't take long," he announced drunkenly, and started to work at his buttons.

"Hey!" she shouted, gathering her robe and pulling back into the corner. "Are you crazy? Jess!" she bellowed toward the door.

Punk, britches down around his ankles, grabbed her by the ankles and dragged her toward him. "Now, you just be quiet, honey," he said through clenched teeth. "Don't you see I love you?"

She slapped at him and struggled, shouting, "You jackass! Jess! Jess!"

But that was the last of it, because Punk simply picked up a figurine and smacked her over the head with it. The figurine went smash and she went still, and Punk opened up her robe—she'd been buck naked, just like he thought, and she had right pretty boobies—and opened up her legs and had his way with her.

He'd been right about it not taking long. She should have listened to him. He figured that if she'd been conscious, she might have enjoyed it.

After, he sat down at her dressing table for a spell, fingering the pots of makeup and smell-nice and rouge, and listening to the show outside, on the stage. And once sufficient time has passed—and since she was still out cold—he did her again.

This time, he left his teeth marks on her booby. Just something for her to remember him by. A ring around that pretty pink rosebud.

He fixed his clothes, and, as an afterthought, grabbed the twelve dollars and eighty-some cents from the tip jar on Mary Jane's dressing table, then left by the rear door. He snagged his old gray pony off the rail and nudged it north, thinking that he'd ride until just before dawn, grab a couple hours of sleep, then move on again. Tucson wasn't that far away. Maybe he'd find him a gal that he wouldn't have to coldcock.

He smiled. He loved them all.

10

After searching the whole night, Cole finally gave up on finding Bob Chavez. He and Tinker and Rolly had scoured the surrounding terrain—Lando's leg was hurting too much to ride, he'd claimed, although he'd ridden right out this morning—and they had come up empty.

And so, at first light, the tired rustlers had begun to push the herd south again.

Cole was wobbling on the edge of deciding that Bob had just plain run out on him. But a couple of things kept him from tumbling entirely. First, Bob hadn't seemed like he was itchy to move on. In fact, a couple of times here recently, he'd talked about how he was going to spend his share of the money.

Besides, a fella didn't just kite out in the middle of the night, now, did he? Especially when he could have done it anytime. Bob would have known that Cole would be pissed, but not pissed enough to do anything about it. It was Bob giving up his share of the money, after all, and the only thing Cole would have to be mad about was being shorthanded for the rest of the drive.

Still, Cole supposed that maybe Bob had his reasons. He had considered foul play, too. In fact, that had been his first thought: that Lando had been up to some dirty business out there, in the dark. But then, why would Lando bother to come back? And what had happened to Bob's body? Lando sure as hell couldn't have dug a grave, not with a busted leg, a wounded shoulder, and a shot-up wrist.

They hadn't found a blasted thing, not even Bob's horse.

Well, Bob had probably just lit out, Cole kept telling himself. When you hired a bunch of stupid, second-class bandits, you were bound to get people who did idiot things for no reason at all. At least, no reason a sane man could figure out.

At the moment, the rustlers were coaxing the herd through a narrow pass. Lando, with his bum leg, had gone through first with Tinker, and Cole and Rolly were bringing up the rear.

They'd managed to put together ninety or ninety-five head out of the original hundred and thirty. It wasn't good, but with Bob long gone, he supposed it would work out about the same. Still, it chapped his butt to think about those other thirty-five or forty head out there: cash money on the hoof, wandering free.

Couldn't be helped, he kept telling himself.

And then he began to wonder if maybe Bob had rounded up those steers and was taking them out in another direction, all by his lonesome.

With a start, he sat up straight in the saddle. Damn that crazy Bob! If he thought he could handle that many beeves all by himself, especially out here, in No Man's Land . . .

No, Cole thought with a shake of his head. He was tired, that was all, tired to the bone, and he was thinking crazy. Bob was too dull to think of making off with that many head of cattle all on his own, and just too plain dumb to pull it off.

Cole sighed and signaled to Rolly, who nodded and pushed the final few head along after the first. Three abreast, that's about all this little old pass could handle.

Falling in together, the two men followed the steers down the narrow chasm.

Hector jogged along after the others, feeling sad. It just came over him at odd moments, no matter how hard he tried to push it away.

There'll be time for this later, he'd think. *You're acting like a fool. Tico wouldn't want you to get yourself killed for him, and neither would Ramona.*

Except that when he thought those things, thought foolishly, stupidly, about what his horse and camel would have wished—as if they could have wished anything at all—it just made him all the sadder. Because he secretly thought that it was true.

He never would have admitted this, not to Slocum or anybody else, even if they dragged him through the cactus at a gallop.

And so he rode along, quietly holding his own private wake.

I'm goin' to be one of those brain-fried old desert rats in a few years, if I don't watch it, Hector thought. *One of those crazy old men who bores everybody silly and spits inside and marries his burro.* And then, after he'd think it, he'd shudder.

But he always watched the trail. That came from years of habit. He watched the places the cattle had walked, watched for the tracks of shod hooves where they emerged briefly from the mess of cattle tracks in the mire and thin mud. He watched the other men from time to time, too, and, somewhat disapprovingly, he watched Connie Nelson.

She was watching Slocum like a hungry harpy watches a rabbit.

*   *   *

Slocum checked the sun, then checked his pocket watch, just to make certain. He'd been right. Ten on the nose.

They had just come into the sieve-like canyon he remembered, and by the looks of it, the rustlers had indeed spent the night here. The ground had been torn up by the nervous hooves of milling cattle.

The rustlers had lost more than a few head, too. Tracks, both cattle and horse, flowed out through the side entrances and over the little valleys, then flowed back in.

They must have been rounding up strays and bringing them back in all night. The whole batch of them—horses, cows, and rustlers—would be good and tired, which could be both a good thing or a bad thing. Tired men had poor reaction times, but tired men were also jumpy as hell.

There was no telling what tired beeves would get up to.

All things considered, maybe it broke about even: no better, no worse, just different.

He heard a horse jogging up beside him, and within seconds Connie Nelson's pretty bay was even with Creole. He nodded an acknowledgment, but that was all.

"Jovial as ever, I see," Connie said, grinning.

Slocum grunted. He liked her. Liked her quite a lot, actually. At least, he liked the press of her lush bosom against her shirt. He'd been secretly waiting all day for one of the straining buttons to just give up and give way.

But she had about the worst timing since Custer galloped into the Little Big Horn after those Indians.

"How's your hip?"

"Some better," he said. It was. "I'll live."

She smirked, although she managed to do it prettily. "Can't tell you how gratified I am to hear that," she said, and abruptly reined her horse away.

Slocum heaved out a little sigh as she jogged off to the west. Women.

Salty Nelson jogged up on the other side of him with his jaw clenched. Probably to keep those store teeth from jiggling right out of his head, Slocum thought.

"How far ahead are they, you think?" Salty asked, once he got his teeth straightened out.

"Not far," replied Slocum. "A couple of hours, maybe three. They're movin' slow."

Salty frowned in disapproval. "So are we."

Slocum said, "We're gainin' on 'em, but I don't want to catch them up until we're out of No Man's Land. Too many nooks and crannies in here."

"Never could figure this goddamn place out," Salty said with a shake of his head and click of his teeth. "Never had much reason to try. Even the damn cows don't wander in here unless they're pushed. Critters might be stupider than a brick wall, but at least they know there ain't no water or fodder for 'em in here."

"You're gonna have to figure it out," Slocum said. "Once we get these rustlers sorted out, I figure you got a whole batch of strays to pick up in here." He nodded at the muddy trail ahead. "They're pushing a few less than they started with."

"Figure that out when I get there," grumbled Salty. "How's that hip of yours?"

The whole damn family was interested, weren't they? Slocum said, "I'll live."

"Don't let Connie bother you, now."

Slocum arched a brow. "Beg pardon?"

"Just don't let her distract you," Salty said, and his big mustache twitched. "I reckon you know what I mean." He paused to adjust his uppers, muttering, "Damn it, anyways." Then he looked over at Slocum and said, "Take good care'a your choppers, Slocum. You remember that. You ain't gonna get another set, leastwise home-growed, once you lose 'em."

Slocum grinned. "I'll remember that, Salty."

"And I mean it about not lettin' Connie's jiggle throw you off track. I don't care what you two get up to later on." He stopped for a second, then said, "All right, I care, I reckon, but there ain't a damn thing I can do about it, though Lord knows I've tried."

Slocum arched a brow, and Salty wearily shook his head. "Just remember, Slocum: I'm the one payin' you for the time bein', and what I'm payin' you for is to get my cows back. And hang the ones what took 'em, if we should get a chance at it. Once you get that done, what you do about that niece of mine is your own business, for better or worse."

Slocum said, "And that's just how I'm proceedin', Salty."

"I'm just tellin' you."

Slocum frowned. "And one time is enough, you old coot."

Salty colored. "Sorry," he said after a moment. "Guess I forgot who I was talkin' to there for a minute."

Slocum softened a little and said, "We're gonna get your cows back, Salty. Quit stewin'."

One more narrow pass and they were out of here, Cole was thinking. One more narrow pass, and he'd never have to go through this hellish maze again. It would be relatively smooth going from here on in. Some low mountains, yes. Some desert, yes. But none of it as treacherous as No Man's Land.

He could see the last pass in the distance. The opening just peeked at him from around the bend. They'd navigated hills and valleys, twisted through canyons great and small, bypassed dead ends and false trails, and they were going to come out all right—due greatly to his own familiarity with No Man's Land, learned through trial and error, and over years. They were almost clear of it.

He hoped he'd never have to see this godforsaken place again as long as he lived.

"Tinker!" he shouted over the noise of the herd.

When Tinker turned in his saddle, Cole pointed up ahead, toward the entrance to the pass. From here, it looked kind of like one of those rock rainbows, kind of like they had up in the northern part of the territory: a natural reddish arch in the stone wall, with nothing beneath and beyond it but black.

He knew that it went through, though. He also knew that they'd have to dismount to go the first hundred feet of her. But then it would open up clear to the sky, and a quarter mile past that, the whole pass would open wide to a vast and grassy plain.

Green again.

Heaven.

Well, almost heaven. The angels—his angel, anyway—lay further south.

He nudged his horse with his heels, scattering the cattle ahead, and rode toward the opening in the rock.

Punk Alvarez had changed his mind about riding up to Tucson.

He'd managed to shake the Tombstone posse, and was just now cooling out his horse—and beginning to breathe easy, himself.

Who would have thought they'd get so goddamn upset about some lousy songbird whore? Hell, she hadn't even been that good a singer, and it hadn't been that good a saloon, just one of those slapped together, half-ass cantinas. Probably be torn down in a year to make room for another assay office. Or a bigger saloon.

But the posse had come on. And come on. And come on. He hadn't got a chance to sleep. Christ, they'd chased him half the night and half the morning, and if he hadn't remembered about that big stretch of rocky ground, he would never have shaken them.

Apparently they knew about that rocky ground, too, because they'd stopped smack at the edge of it. And while he watched through his spyglass—having veered off at an angle and climbed up into the hills, lickety-split—they sat their horses, discussing something, and then they finally turned around and headed back south, toward town and coffee and the comfort of their beds.

He'd be damned it he could figure it out. Maybe they'd hit the edge of their jurisdiction or something. Course, that wouldn't have stopped a few marshals he'd known, no sir. Or maybe they'd had better things to do. After all, it wasn't like he'd killed the girl. He'd just had a little fun, that was all.

Or maybe they figured to just give it up and not waste any time trying to track him over rocky ground.

Punk figured that was likely it.

He also figured that they'd wire Tucson to be on the lookout for him, and belatedly kicked himself—mentally, at least—for having mentioned his name to the bartender. Dumb, dumb, dumb.

Well, he couldn't know that he'd get a yen for that girl, Whatshername, now could he?

Mary Jane, that was it.

She had her nerve, enticing him that way.

They oughta put a posse on her, that's what they should do.

And then he grinned, picturing a whole dang posse pumping away at Miss Mary Jane Crabtree while she hollered, "Jess! Jess!"

A woman shouldn't be in a business where the whole of her goal was to entice menfolk, he thought as he stepped up on his tired gray. She shouldn't strut the stage and show her wares, not unless she wanted somebody to come calling, wanted somebody to take her up on what she was advertising.

No, sir.

Punk kicked the gray into a walk and began to climb up through the rocky hills, heading in a general northwest direction. Maybe he'd head over toward Silverbell. Silverbell was nice, if you didn't mind that you could practically see through the hotel walls and the gals all had Cupid's Itch and the whiskey was two dollars a glass.

Well, no. Thinking about the price of whiskey put him right off Silverbell. He didn't have much, and he had to stretch it.

He'd just figure it out as he went along.

11

At about that same time, and not too far to the southwest in the dusty town of Pozo Artesiano, Gordo Guardado became a free man.

This wasn't because of any kindness on Sheriff Bill Ploughshare's part. No, it was primarily because Ploughshare, being occupied across town with a couple of gun-wielding rowdies, had left his new deputy, Anson Foley, in charge of the jail. And Anson Foley had made the mistake of letting one Charlene "Charlie Bee Sting" Thacker—a worn out and haggard little prostitute whose only saving grace was that she had the prettiest rosebud mouth west of El Paso—into the jail to see Gordo.

Charlene being none-too-bright, Anson Foley being all-too-green, and Gordo being Gordo, the escape took all of fifteen seconds. Gordo locked Charlene and the unconscious deputy in a cell, and the last thing he heard, as he left the town jail by the back door, was Charlie Bee Sting complaining, "Dad-blame it, Gordo, I thought you liked me!"

Gordo had always known that she'd come in handy one day.

Old habits died hard. Keeping to the shadows, he

walked up to the Double Deuce Saloon and snagged another horse that wasn't his—a right handsome dun— off the rail and jogged it nonchalantly—so as not to draw attention—until he reached the city limits, then dug spurs into its clay-colored flanks and headed east.

Easy as pie.

Slocum sat his horse just to the south of the place where No Man's Land ended and the good grazing country began, his spyglass to his eye. He could see the place where the rain had stopped, a hard line in the tall grass.

That was Arizona Territory for you. Crazy weather. Once, it had rained buckets on the back half of his horse and the front half had remained dry as a bone. He'd paced it, made a game of it, and kept the front half dry for a good five minutes before the wind changed direction and he got good and soaked.

He glassed the distance. The cows were out there, all right, a brown and white and black and white mass cutting through the center of the plain. They moved slowly, tiredly. He knew they'd find a reserve of energy if something spooked them, though.

Salty Nelson waited impatiently at his side. "Well?" Salty prompted. "How many?"

"Riders?" Slocum collapsed the glass. "Four."

Salty smiled nastily. "We've got the bastards, then."

"Not quite yet," replied Slocum, and gestured the others in closer. "Now, I figure these cattle are pretty spooky, but they're pretty damned tired, too. I don't think they'll go far, and this plain is naturally configured to convince 'em to stick halfway close. So we're just gonna go in and get the cows, nothing frilly. Hector, you and Lenny cut round to the west. Stay out of sight. You boys," he said to the other two hands Salty had brought along, "swing wide and go around the east. Me and Salty'll bring up the rear."

Hector nodded approvingly. "A 'Y.' I like it."

"Nobody do nothin' until you hear me fire," Slocum added. "And for God's sake, pick your targets careful. Don't need you boys shootin' each other up."

Hector and the hands reined their horses away and sauntered off in their respective directions, but Connie stayed. "What do you mean, 'me and Salty'?"

"Just what I said," Slocum growled. "You stay put. We'll pick you up on our way back."

She pulled herself up and pressed her lips together. "The hell you will!"

"Now, damn it, Connie . . . ," Salty began.

"Shut up, Uncle Salty. These cows are as much mine as yours. Well, almost. And I've got just as much right as anybody else to—"

As one, the two men shouted, *"No!"*

"I mean it, Connie," Salty threatened with a click of his teeth.

"Listen to your uncle if you won't listen to me," Slocum said. "Lead's gonna be flyin' fast and furious out there, and there's no telling what them beeves'll do. Might turn contrary on us. Somebody's got to be in one piece to pick up the chucks if we all get trampled to squash."

Connie brightened somewhat, likely at the thought of them slashed and pummeled by flying cloven hooves. She probably thought it would serve them right.

Salty muttered, "Don't know why you have to put things so goddamn colorful, Slocum . . ."

"You gonna stay?" Slocum asked the girl.

Connie snapped the edge of one stiff hand to her forehead in a crisp salute. "Yes, sir," she said sarcastically. "Oh, yessirree Bob and pass the biscuits, Mighty Slocum."

Under his breath, Slocum muttered, "Brother." If she

hadn't been so damn beautiful, he would have had half a mind to slap her.

But he motioned toward Salty, and the two of them began slowly to move down into the grassland and toward the distant herd. Slocum took a quick look over his shoulder just to make sure Connie had stayed where she was told.

She had.

"Don't let any important parts get squashed, Slocum," Connie called after him.

"My brother should'a drowned her at birth," Salty grouched.

Slocum allowed himself a little smile. "Aw, I think she's kind of cute, Salty."

"Cute like a rattlesnake," Salty grumbled.

Punk Alvarez rode up from the southeast just in time to see the show.

He'd been traveling slow, half-asleep in the saddle, letting the horse's plodding movement rock him gently while he considered such things as pretty women and whiskey, and just what the chances were of getting his hands on either one in Pozo Artesiano, when the horse jerked its head up.

"What is it this time, you old bangtail?" Punk asked, annoyed. And then he looked out, between the horse's pricked ears, and saw what the horse was looking at.

Cattle, a whole mess of them, well off in the distance. And riders. Some with the herd, it looked like, but some a lot closer to him, shadowing it.

Punk wasn't too smart, but he was nobody's fool, and he got right down off that horse and quickly led it behind a tall clump of prickly pear, then got out his spyglass and had a look.

The herd was in high grass, nearly withers-deep, and had moved just about even with him by that time. The shadowing riders, two of them riding abreast down a shallow gulch, had moved a little ahead of it. There looked to be another couple of boys trailing, nice and easy. He could just make them out over the tall grass. They were moving a little faster, though, now that he was watching them.

He swung the glass back and tried to pick out the riders with the herd. As far as he knew, this might be the bunch of boys Lando was supposed to meet up with. The boys Punk himself was supposed to meet up with, too, if that idiot, Gordo, hadn't bollixed things up by swiping that Appy.

Except right at the moment, it appeared that somebody was about to swipe those cows right out from under them. Punk was actually sort of happy that Gordo had taken a fancy to that Appy. At least he wasn't out there, about to be ambushed.

Unless Lando was with the riders circling the herd, that was. Then again, he might not be out there at all. This could be a totally different bunch of beeves, he reckoned.

It was a little too complicated for Punk's tired brain to figure out, and he had just lowered the glass in order to give a good scratch to the back of his head when all hell broke loose.

At the first shot, he brought the spyglass up so fast that he hit himself in the nose with it and swore under his breath. Three more shots had split daylight before he finished cursing and brought the spyglass to bear again.

By then, the cattle had bolted. They were going every which way, and there were riders caught up in the center of it. The men from the outskirts had moved in, and Punk saw somebody go down in a roil of skittish cattle. He couldn't tell which batch of men he was with.

A dust cloud had quickly risen over the tall grass and brush, and Punk had to dive to one side to avoid a few head of steers that emerged from it not thirty feet from where he was standing. They galloped past, going full out.

More shots. He didn't know how they could see what they were shooting at in there! He sure as hell couldn't see anything anymore, and he got to thinking that maybe he'd better get while the getting was good. That would beat everything wouldn't it, to get himself hanged for a cattle thief the one time he hadn't actually stolen any, but had just stumbled onto the scene?

He smacked a palm over his spyglass, collapsing it, and hurried the few steps to the prickly pear and his pony. He jammed a foot in the stirrup, hopped up, and dug his heels into the gray. It wasn't until he reached the line of hills he'd come from that he reined in the horse and took another long look through the spyglass.

There was cows all over the place. They must have been tired, because none of them had run too far—just bolted, got clear, and stopped. But they dotted the wide plain and grazed in scattered clusters of five and six here, two and three there.

And farther out, near the place he'd come from, the settling dust revealed three men down, three riderless horses, and six more men, standing around and poking at the bodies.

Punk sure wished he knew who was who.

He swung the glass to the south, toward the distant line of hills that bounded this wide plain, and saw a thin billow of dust in the distance, dust which could only be created by a galloping horse. He smiled a little. One fellow had got away, at least. Punk always rooted for the underdog.

And he got to thinking that maybe it might behoove him to follow that man. He'd about convinced himself that the boys with the herd were rustlers—the brands on those cows that had skittered past him looked raw and brand-new. Couldn't be more than a week old, at best.

And besides, he reckoned he was better off partnered up with somebody. Punk was a follower, not a leader, and he knew it. Be nice to have somebody to tell him what to do again. Besides, it might be Lando that had got away. Now, wouldn't that be something!

So he set out, keeping to the edge of the hills, and began to skirt the plain, moving ever southward.

Slocum nudged a body with his toe. "This one's dead, too," he said.

"Good," spat Salty Nelson. "The government oughta pay a bounty on these vermin, same as they pay on wolves."

"Well, we'll haul him back," Slocum replied. "No tellin'. There might be paper on him."

Orville, one of Salty's hands, had bent to the corpse and was busily going through his pockets. Grunting, he produced a battered wallet and handed it up to Salty.

"Ticket stub," said Salty, eyes squinted as he went through it. "A dollar and twenty-seven cents—no, twenty-eight. 'Nother ticket stub. Piece of yellow ribbon . . . Here we go. A letter." He unfolded it and peered at the address on the envelope. "Fella was named Rolly Clum. You ever heared of him?"

Slocum shook his head. The cattle had trampled the grass flat here—and for quite a ways around—and he turned to the side, toward a distant cluster of men. "Is yours dead?" he shouted.

Hector stepped away from the group, cupped his hands around his mouth, and shouted back, "Deader'n a doornail. And you ain't gonna believe who he is."

Slocum shouted back, "Lando Reese?"

There was a pause before Hector shouted back, "Dammit, Slocum!"

Slocum grinned. He was glad that the murdering

Lando was dead, gladder than he could have ever impressed on Hector. Course, Hector had his reasons to be joyous, too. Beneath his breath, Slocum said, "I didn't exactly get him myself, Joey, but at least I presided over it." He hoped the boy would rest easy now.

He and Salty turned toward the sound of approaching hooves to see Connie jogging up. Nonchalantly, she reined in her mount, leaned down, crossed her forearms over her saddle horn, and asked, "Is it safe now for us helpless females?"

Salty closed his eyes and worked his jaw muscles.

Slocum said, "It's safe. You wanna throw this boy back on his horse and secure him?"

Connie's brows shot up, and Slocum laughed. When she colored hotly, he said, "Well, you're the one who wants to be treated like one of the men."

She snorted. "Not all the time, Slocum."

"Promises, promises," he replied.

"Just . . . just stop it!" roared Salty. He was bright red. "Just hold off and that nasty talk, all right? At least have the decency to jabber like that outta my earshot."

Connie reached down and patted his shoulder. "There, there, Uncle Salty."

He sighed heavily, but at least he didn't say anything more. A good thing, because Slocum was fighting back laughter. By God, this Connie was a piece of work all right.

Then she said, "I don't suppose anybody cares that one of them got clean away."

Slocum answered first. "I saw him go, but I was sort of busy right at the moment. What do you say, Salty?"

Slocum had hoped Salty would just shrug and say good riddance, but instead, he said, "I hired you to get my rustlers, Slocum. You ain't finished the job yet."

Well, there went Slocum's plans of an evening with Connie under the stars. After all, Salty was paying him five hundred to take care of this little rustler problem, and any man who offered him that much money—especially for something that was turning out not to be much work at all—was very much the boss.

So he nodded and said, "Your call, Salty," and stuck a foot in his stirrup.

Salty swept off his hat and banged his thigh with it. "Not right now, goddamn it! Somebody's gotta help gather up these dang cows!"

Slocum took his foot back out of the stirrup and leaned against Creole. "You already got a bunch of boys," he said, his brow cocked.

"And I also got cows all over the damned place," Salty railed. "Plus, I got three fellers to pack up and carry back up to Tucson. Now, I figure that we can take care'a most of that, but you are, by God, gonna stick around until we get those blasted cows bunched back up and get these bodies ready to travel."

Having spent most of his fury, Salty paused to adjust his uppers, muttered, "Damn it, anyway," then said to Slocum, "You can light out after him in the morning. He won't be movin' fast, I don't think. I'm pretty sure I clipped him."

"You're the boss," Slocum said as he stuck a foot in his stirrup. This time he made it all the way up onto the horse, and by the time he did, Salty had a hand to his chest.

Connie was digging in her shirt pocket, and pulled out a small vial of pills, which she handed down to Salty. "Take one, Uncle Salty. Now."

Scowling, he brushed away her hand.

"I mean it," she insisted. "You take one right this instant, or I swear I'll throw you to the ground and make you take it."

He grudgingly took the bottle, dumped a pill into his hand, and popped it in his mouth.

"If I've told you once," she said softly, "I've told you a thousand times. Quit getting so goddamned mad. You got three out of four of those bastards. You ought to be happy."

He handed the vial back and grunted at her.

"Now go sit down. Somewhere in the shade. I'm serious."

Slocum had observed this little scene in silence, but after Salty walked away, he asked, "His heart?"

Connie nodded. "Stubborn old bull. It just kills him to take those pills, like it's a sign of weakness or something. If I wasn't along to force him . . ."

Connie was looking better to Slocum all the time, but he had cattle to gather. "You'll keep an eye on him?" he asked.

"Always do," she said.

Slocum reined Creole away and jogged him over to where Hector was standing. The boys were already tying Lando's battered corpse across his saddle. He had been pretty busted up to begin with, Slocum thought, but after a few dozen head of beeves had trampled him, he was looking pretty damned ratty.

Hector stuck a thumb over his shoulder, toward the south. "What about that one?"

"Tomorrow, I guess," Slocum replied. "Ol' Salty's got his knickers in a twist about his steers."

Hector mounted up, too, and they rode out toward the east, where a knot of about ten head had congregated. On their way toward the cattle, they passed the third rustler they'd killed. He'd been badly trampled, and there was no telling what he had once looked like. Slocum said, "You check this one yet?"

Hector nodded. "Tinker Reese. Brother to Lando."

"Small world."

"Yup."

"Believe I've seen paper on him," Slocum offered.

"Well," Hector said philosophically, "if there's a reward, the cows are gonna get it. Couldn't find a hole in him. Guess his horse just reared and dumped him, and the cattle did the rest."

Slocum studied his reins. "I can think of better ways to die."

12

Cole Strait made it almost six miles before he toppled slowly from his horse. The horse, which had been ambling with little direction from Cole for the past half hour or so, simply stopped and gratefully began to crop grass.

Cole watched him through bleary eyes. He didn't know how much blood he'd lost, but he figured that it wouldn't take much more to kill him.

He was all alone. His men were dead, the lousy shitheels. They should have seen trouble coming. He hadn't, but at least he had the excuse of having been riding out in front of the herd. They'd come from behind, hadn't they? Maybe from the sides, too, come to think of it.

But his men should have seen something. The grass was tall, but not *that* damn tall!

He'd have to hire better men next time, he thought, and then he reminded himself that there wouldn't be a next time. He'd never see Conchita again, his beautiful Conchita of the flashing obsidian eyes and the smooth hips and the silky brown skin. He'd never get to Paso Pedregoso. The peasants there would never learn what had become of him.

It struck him as ironic that the one group of people who trusted him, believed in him, cared for him, would come to think that he had deserted them. In truth, in all the world they were the only ones he wanted to get back to. He would have died to get back to Conchita and her little white adobe house, back to Paso Pedregoso, with its small farms and happy peasants. Now it seemed he was just going to die.

His vision was swimming. He tried to shift his position, to make himself a little more comfortable on the rocky ground, but found he was too weak.

He closed his eyes and thought about Tinker Reese. He'd seen him go down in the middle of all those cows. There'd been no question of getting to him. He'd known Tinker was a dead man the moment he fell. He felt terrible sad about that boy, mighty sad that he had to die that way.

Well, he was going to join up with Tinker soon enough.

"Don't draw on me, there, mister," said a voice. "I'm comin' in."

That was funny. Cole hadn't expected the Lord—or Satan, either, for that matter—to be concerned about firearms. He said, "Do with me what you will."

Or maybe Cole just thought he said it. He could no longer feel what his body was doing. He just felt like he was floating, floating over the grassland, floating over the hills, floating up into the sun.

"Jeez, you done got yourself shot up good," said the voice again. It sounded so far away.

And then a hand roughly turned him over. *That,* he felt, and it rocked him far enough up into lucidity that he suddenly realized he wasn't dead. At least, not yet. The inside of his eyelids burning bright with the light of the dying sun and far to heavy to open, he managed to move his lips just enough to mumble, "Who . . . who are you?"

Fingers clumsily prodded his wound. "Reckon I'm the feller who's gonna save your hide. Ain't all that bad, so don't you worry. You sure lost a lot of blood, though. You want a drink of water?"

Cole felt himself nod.

He still hadn't the strength to open his eyes, but he heard the man get up.

"Name's Punk," said the voice. "Punk Alvarez. And I reckon, by the look of you, that you're Cole Strait. That right?"

There was a pause, during which Cole made no acknowledgment whatsoever, and then Punk said, "Well, I don't reckon I'd admit it to a stranger, neither, if I was you. But if it sets your mind to ease any, I was supposed to come work for you, me and Gordo, 'cept Gordo thieved a horse and Lando cut us loose. Lando Reese, that is. He one of the dead ones back there?"

With the greatest of efforts, Cole cracked his eyes open. He saw the legs of a gray horse—which were immediately blotted out by a giant belly, buttons straining, and the squat man attached to it. The man shoved a canteen in his face.

Cole took a grateful drink, and his eyes fluttered closed again.

"Well, reckon we'd best get to it," Punk's voice said.

Cole figured he'd be dead inside the hour. God was toying with him, that was all. He'd sent this buffoon to "help" him, when all he was likely to help him into was his grave.

"Now, this here's gonna hurt you some," Punk continued. "Ain't got no liquor to ease it, and I'm mighty sorry for that. But don't you holler none, you got me? If'n you holler, I'm gonna have to knock you out. We ain't all that far from them boys what put the lead in you in the first place. Here," he said, and Cole felt something rough and nasty go into his mouth. A stick.

"Bite down on that," said Punk. "Best I could find. Now, hold still."

The pain began anew.

By the time Slocum and his men had rounded up and bunched the cattle, there was still a good hour of daylight left. Salty Nelson showed absolutely no interest in letting Slocum ride out after the single escaped rustler, though.

"I told you, I got him," Salty insisted. "Saw him near to lurch right off his pony when the slug took him. There's no sense in you ridin' out, what with it coming dark pretty soon. He's likely dead, anyhow."

Slocum sighed. "Then what's the point of my goin' after him at all?"

" 'Cause I wanna see the body, that's why," Salty insisted grouchily. "I wanna haul him into town with these other deceased miscreants. I'm payin' you. Do what I say, you hear?"

Well, there was no arguing with Salty when he had the bit between his teeth, so Slocum just shrugged and got on with the business of settling Creole in for the night. He just hoped that Salty was right, and that he'd only be going out there to pick up a body.

Hector volunteered to ride along with him. "I'm likely not goin' to get paid a wood nickel for this deal, anyhow," he told Slocum later, by the picket line. Slocum had already fed and watered Creole, and rubbed him down good.

"Might's well finish it," Hector continued. "Got nothing else real pressin' to do."

Slocum folded Creole's empty feed bag and stuck it under his arm. "Well, you're gonna get paid, one way or the other, even if I have to pay you out of what Salty pays me. I already told you that. You know, Hector, this whole thing would've turned out a lot different if you hadn't been along."

"If I hadn't let that son of a bitch, Lando, get the better of me, you mean," Hector muttered. "Let him kill my camel and kill my horse. I swear, I ain't worth shit."

"I'm sure sorry about that, Hector," Slocum said kindly. He wasn't sure about camels, but he certainly knew what it was to lose a horse you were fond of.

"Yeah, yeah," Hector said, and then his shoulders drooped. "Aw, hell. I'm sorry, Slocum. I reckon you understand better than most." He straightened his shoulders again. "Well, we got two of the bastards, anyway. Reckon the third one—that Punk feller—has gone past the point of ever findin' him."

Slocum nodded. "Suppose you're right. But two out of three ain't bad, Hector. It ain't bad at all."

Night was almost on them by this time. A cookfire had been built and Slocum, all the way down at the picket line, could already smell the aromas of supper cooking. That Connie might have been a real pistol but, by God, she cooked like she was born to nothing but the kitchen. He was looking forward to dinner. He was also looking forward to what might happen later on, after everyone else was asleep.

Hector read his mind. "You'd best be careful about that gal," he said.

"Careful about her, or about Salty?" Slocum asked with a grin.

"Both," Hector replied. "I swear, Slocum, I have never in my life met me a feller who's more of a magnet for the ladies. *And* for trouble."

Slocum shrugged. "It's a gift."

"My ass," muttered Hector.

From the fire, Connie, in silhouette, stood up and hollered, "Come and get it!"

Slocum planned to.

* * *

She came to him after eleven, stepping quietly over the sleeping forms of the hands. He had picked a spot well away from the fire, well away from the others, and he watched her as she came closer.

She was wrapped in a blanket from head to toe. Nothing showed of her but her boots below and her head above. When she drew near, he threw back his blanket and made a place for her beside him. She'd been teasing him for so long that he'd gone hard as a rock when he saw her stand up, and her journey across the campsite had nearly put him in pain.

She stopped, standing over him, and looked down—first at his face, and then at the straining bulge in his britches.

"You were pretty sure I'd come, weren't you?" she asked. The light was behind her, and he couldn't read her face.

"Yup," he replied.

She was silent for a moment, and then she let the blanket drop in a puddle at her feet. She was completely nude, save for the boots on her feet, and she just stood there, looking at him.

He swallowed hard. Round, full breasts with upturned nipples floated above a tiny waist. Her hips were slim yet feminine, and slid smoothly into long, shapely legs that he wanted wrapped around him in the worst way.

And then she pointed toward his crotch and said, "You'd best give that big ol' monster some breathing room before he strangles, Slocum."

"Yes'm," he said, holding his hand up to her. "Maybe you could give me a little help with that?"

She propped her hands on her slim flare of hips and tipped her head. "Hm. Suppose I could."

She turned then, and he caught just a glimpse of the delta of dark curls at the juncture of her thighs. They were already glistening with moisture. She'd been waiting too long for this, too.

He pulled her down to him, running his hands over her naked body without fanfare. Her skin was impossibly silky and without flaw. He cupped her high, firm breasts, lush and plump, and tweaked the nipples. She moaned low in her throat and whispered, "Your hip still hurting you?"

"What hip?" he said, intent on her breasts. He brushed a kiss over one peak.

"I thought we'd never have a chance at this, Slocum," she whispered, just before she kissed him.

Her fingers worked feverishly at his buttons, and before he knew it, she had freed him and held him in both of her hands. "Dear God," she murmured urgently. "You're enormous! Do me fast, Slocum. Fast and just as hard as you can."

It was exactly his thought, and he quickly shoved his britches down, rolled over on top of her, and entered her silky warmth in one smooth stroke, burying himself to the hilt.

She made a small, mewling sound and hungrily bucked her hips up toward his. There was no time for soft, lovers' caresses, no time for nuance. They were animals, besotted by rut.

He began to pound into her almost savagely, and she answered each thrust with an enthusiastic tilt of her pelvis and buck of her hips; with her nails, which dug and clawed the flesh of his back; and with her teeth, which raked at his shoulders.

And within moments, he felt her stiffen with a gigantic climax and heard her take in air in a backwards scream. Seconds later, he felt nothing but the rush of his own teeming sensations as he came, too.

They lay there for a moment: her nails still poised to

rake, Slocum still inside her. The only sound was of their heavy panting.

And then she said, still gasping, "That was . . . a lovely . . . start."

13

Punk Alvarez was on the move.

He traveled slowly and carefully through the night, leading Cole Strait's horse—with Cole thrown over its back. He heard Cole groan every now and then, but he paid it no mind. Cole would be hurting a good bit, but he wasn't going to die.

Punk wanted to get to Jaguar Springs before he stopped for the night. Going at this rate, he figured it would take him another hour or so—an hour and a half, tops. He'd already been traveling for nearly four hours, ever since he'd pulled the slug out of Cole's back and packed the wound. He hadn't seen hide nor hair of those fellas who'd snatched back Cole's herd, and they likely weren't following, but he wasn't going to take any chances, nosirree.

He swung to the left to avoid another good sized thicket of those little sticker bushes, then rolled himself a smoke. Lighting it, he congratulated himself once again on his good luck. Finding a man like Cole Strait clear out here, in the middle of dog-squat nothing! Why, with Cole's brain to guide him, he'd likely be a rich man inside six weeks!

Lando had mentioned his brother was riding with Cole—the brother they were supposed to meet up with (until Gordo had pulled that show-off stunt and made Lando mad), and the brother that Punk figured currently lay up north a ways with Lando, killed deader than a doornail. Lando hadn't said much about Cole, but he didn't have to. At least, not to Punk. He was already well-acquainted with Cole's reputation.

He'd heard that Cole had been some big Reb hero in the war, till the Rebs found out he was thieving their gold shipments. One, anyway. That got him stripped of his rank and thrown in prison, until he tunneled his way to freedom with a couple of buddies. In the intervening years, Cole Strait had robbed banks and held up coaches and rustled cattle, always in Southern states, and always getting clean away, slick as an eel down a chute.

Punk shook his head. Surely a man like this was worth saving. Hell, he was charmed! Leastwise, he'd never got caught except for the army deal, and that had been a real long time ago. Why, you couldn't hardly count it!

Punk figured to let a little of that luck rub off on him.

He finished his quirlie and nearly tossed it to the ground before he caught himself. He slid one boot out of the stirrup, carefully ground the cigarette out on the underside of his heel, and then tossed the remains to the desert floor. Once, he'd nearly burnt down a whole county—and himself along with it—with a tossed butt, and he wasn't going to repeat the error.

He was out of the grassland now, and traveling over increasingly rugged terrain. Sparse brush had replaced the meager grazing land from which he and Cole had come, and he knew that if he could have seen them, there'd be low hummocks of rocks up ahead, in the distance. In them he'd find Jaguar Springs.

It was a place that he and Lando and Gordo had stopped a few times before, usually on the way to or from Pozo Artesiano. You went threading through the rocks—giant boulders, really—and if you knew where you were going, you'd find yourself in a little hollow, like a cup in the land, with those big, lumpy rocks all the way around a flat, gravelly bottom. There was just enough room for three men to build a fire and bed down, and to tether their horses just far enough away that the damn beasts wouldn't shit all over them at night.

And, of course, there was Jaguar Springs. It was over at the edge of the cup, nestled under a rock, and just enough water bubbled up—before it sank down and disappeared again—that a man could fill a coffeepot. He could fill quite a few coffeepots if he waited long enough.

The water there was sweet and clear and like no other, and Punk was already licking his lips. He figured to dump all the water from their canteens and give it to the horses. It wouldn't be wasted. But that good spring water was sure as shooting going to fill up his canteens, every last one.

Too bad there was no whiskey to go with it. Now, that was something the Lord should have invented: a whiskey spring.

He had plenty of grub, and he figured to just stay at the spring for a day or two and let Cole start to heal up. It was a good hiding place. He pictured himself and Cole discussing what sorts of nefarious business they'd get up to, all the cash money they were going to make, and all the women they'd have.

Punk smiled. He was looking forward to it.

Slocum shuddered and sank back on his blankets, holding Connie, who was recuperating from her second orgasm of the evening. Well, Slocum, too. This time, she had opened her mouth and started to let out a yell that would have awakened not only the camp, but startled every hungry cat and coyote within a square mile. Slocum had clamped a hand over her mouth just in time, and she'd bitten him for his trouble.

He gave it a shake and peered at it again through the darkness. The skin wasn't broken, but it sure as hell was dented.

"I do that?" Connie whispered.

Slocum brushed a kiss over her brow. "You sure did. Reckon it's in better shape than my back, though."

She sighed, and then smiled softly. "Sorry. What can I tell you, Slocum? You just bring out the animal in me."

He chuckled. "Guess so. And whatever kind it is, it sure has claws."

"It has other things, too," she whispered. Taking his wounded hand in hers, she curled it over her breast. It was warm and soft, deliciously firm and weighty in his hand, and he let the nipple slip between the knuckles of his first and second fingers. He gave it a little squeeze that turned into a soft pinch.

She smiled and made a little sound. "That's my boy," she murmured. "Been a long time for me. Too long, if you couldn't tell."

"Oh, I could."

"Did we wake anybody up?"

"It's all right," he whispered, and dipped his head to take her other nipple into his mouth. The first two times had been so fast and furious that he wanted to take the time to enjoy her body. Not that he hadn't enjoyed it before, but he wanted to spend a little time petting her, playing with her, enjoying the sight and smell and feel of her.

She sighed when he sucked the nipple between his lips, and moaned when he rolled it between his teeth. Her hand went to the back of his head, urging him on, and as he began to suckle her in earnest, he felt her other hand come to rest on his wrist, coaxing him to play more roughly with her other nipple.

He obliged happily.

Her hands moved then, while he nursed at her, gliding down his body, lingering along the hard plains of his chest and back, tracing old scars, circling his belly button, sweeping down the small of his back and curling over his buttocks.

One of her hands slid to his groin and took hold of him. He felt himself swelling at her touch as she began to manipulate him gently, so gently, and he slid his free hand down her side, down the dip of her waist, over impossibly silky skin, and up again to her hip.

Her thigh immediately raised up, lifting until it was propped on the point of his hip, and he needed no further invitation. He slipped his hand over the flatness of her belly and past the moist curls below it to part her outer lips. He touched the warm, wet, satiny flesh within.

"Slocum . . . ," she whispered as he nibbled and sucked at her breast. "Slocum . . ." as he slid two fingers inside her. And "Oh Slocum, Oh God . . ." as his thumb found that secret nub of flesh and began to caress it.

He was swelling bigger and bigger beneath her hand, but the next time he mounted her he wanted to take his time. And time was something she wasn't going to give him, not in her state of excitement. She was already pushing her hips toward his hand, already arching her back to pushing her nipple deeper into his mouth.

So he began to slide his fingers slowly in and out of her, all the while keeping up his thumb's ministrations, and those of his mouth at her breast.

The point of her nipple was like a pebble against his tongue, a hard, sweet pebble, and he teased it, nipped it, lapped at it, then pulled away to nuzzle and kiss the underside of her breast before he returned to its center. And all the while he petted and squeezed her other breast, tugging at the nipple, deftly twisting it, while his left hand—now sodden with her moisture—continued to tickle her, tease her, inflame her.

And then he felt her stiffen again in a tremendous convulsion that lifted half her body off the blankets, and he kissed her and swallowed her scream.

At last she flopped back on the blankets, eyes closed, mouth open, panting. He wasted no time. Parting her legs, he mounted her again. He pulled her knees up until they wrapped his waist, and then he sank into her. She was still pulsing from her climax, and as he began to move in her, he found the feeling of those rhythmically trembling walls incredibly exciting.

He moved slowly at first, almost leisurely, letting the tickle in his groin build gradually to a quiet buzz. He dipped his head to lap at her breasts, her collarbones. He kissed her long and sweet, then passionately, then sweet again. And all the time, his meter quickened, his thrusts deepened. And she began to move with him, sharing his urgency.

Raising her legs even higher up his sides, she locked her ankles behind his back. She gripped his upper arms, her nails digging into his flesh as if she were drowning and he were a life preserver.

The buzz in his groin turned into a fiery thing, and he began to pump his hips for all he was worth. He raised himself from his elbows to his hands so that he could watch her breasts jiggle and shake with each thrust. Deeper and deeper he went, faster, more savage, as she clung to him, making small, animal sounds in the back of her throat.

And then the heat in his loins burst into a fiery ball of flame, then a surge of molten lava that spilled and spilled and spilled.

Spent at last, he eased himself down upon her. She

had finished, too, although he couldn't be certain when, and she was gasping for air.

He couldn't remember if she'd cried out, but a quick glance up toward the campfire showed him no moving bodies. They hadn't woken anyone.

Slipping free, he rolled to the side. The warm air was like ice on his cock, and he pulled the edge of the blanket up to cover and warm himself, then rolled back partway to gently kiss Connie's lips.

Her eyes slitted open, and a catlike smile curled her mouth. "You're really something, cowboy," she whispered.

"You, too, darlin'," he said, stroking her temple. "I just aim to please."

They were both sweating, and she shivered. He reached across her and pulled the top blanket, the one she'd worn when she first walked down to him, over them both.

"Thanks," she said.

"Welcome, ma'am," he answered in mock seriousness, and tucked it in behind her. "What do you say we grab some shut-eye?"

Beneath the blanket, her hand slid over his chest and came to rest on an old knife scar. "Ordinarily, I'd smack you for going to sleep," she said teasingly, "except that you plumb wore me out."

He chuckled. "Might say the same for you."

Her fingers traced the scar up and down. "You've been hurt a lot. So many scars."

"It's all right," he said, his eyes closing. "Nothin' killed me yet."

He heard her snort, and then there was a pause. "Slocum?"

"Yes?"

"All those things they say about you . . . They're true, aren't they?"

He opened one eye. "Depends on what they said. Let's talk about this in the mornin', sugar."

"I think they are," she said, ignoring him. "I figured, well, you know how reputations are. The farther they get from the source, the bigger and wilder they get. But yours? I think it was right on the money."

Sleepily, he slid an arm around her shoulders, letting his hand drop so that it rested on one of those world-class breasts of hers. He yawned. "In the mornin', baby."

"All right, pet" was the last thing he heard before he nodded off to sleep.

Far away at the campfire, Hector lay in his blankets staring grimly up at the stars.

Lord, how many times were those two going to do it, anyway? They had him so itchy that he was about to quite literally come in his britches. Sound carried pretty damn well out here, and he had counted four times that they had done it.

Except that it was quiet now. It had been quiet for maybe ten minutes. He supposed they were just catching their damned breaths. Except that after another five minutes passed and there was still no noise, he began to think that maybe something had happened to them. He surely would have heard voices by this time, even if old Slocum had finally run out of steam.

He should go down there and take a look, that's what he should do. Except, what if they were fine and they were awake? Boy howdy, he'd never live that down!

But then, mayhap that last fellow, the one that had galloped off, had come back. Maybe Salty hadn't shot him as good as he'd thought, and he'd sneaked in and done them mischief, and was this minute sneaking up on the camp, thinking to murder them all in their bedrolls.

Hector thought about this good and hard, and finally

decided that he'd best chance it and go have a look-see. At least his aching cock had dwindled in size enough that he thought he could stand up.

Orville hadn't had that problem. True, two of Salty's boys were far away, watching over the herd, but he'd seen a hand moving beneath Orville's blanket—a cowboy pretending to be asleep and snoring while he played with his pecker. Everybody had heard the moans and sounds from Slocum's private little wilderness boudoir. No, just him and Orville, he corrected himself. Salty Nelson had been softly sawing wood the whole dang time.

Unlike Orville, Hector hadn't given in to the urge, no sir, although now he was wondering why he hadn't.

He was just starting to sit up, throw back his blanket, and reach for his holster, when he saw a cloaked figure coming toward the camp from Slocum's bed site. For a second, he was certain that it was the escaped rustler, but then he realized the figure was far too slim. He settled back in his blankets and slitted his eyes nearly closed.

It was Connie, all right. He watched as she walked to her bedroll, across the fire from his. And then she dropped her blanket.

Naked! Naked as the day she was born, except for her boots. He felt himself stiffen to attention again, and bit the inside of his cheek.

Silently, she began to dress again, and despite the pounding weasel in his britches, Hector held himself very still as she gradually clothed every inch of that glorious body.

It was a damn shame, he thought, a goddamn shame. There ought to be a law that any woman as beautiful as Connie Nelson had to be naked twenty-four hours a day. Had to do her chores naked, her marketing naked, had to go to the damned bank and feed store without a stitch.

It would sure do wonders for the whole male population of the country.

He watched as she lay down and got comfortable, and then and only then did he unbutton his britches and let the weasel loose. He was so swollen and aching and blue-balled that he barely had to touch himself before he came.

It was a good thing that he and Slocum were riding out first thing in the morning, he thought as he wiped his hand on the blanket, then buttoned himself back up. He didn't think he could stand another night of this.

14

Slocum reined his horse in and stared down at the ground, waiting for Hector to catch up with him. Hector had been uncharacteristically quiet this morning, and riding a good length or two behind so as to make conversation impossible, but Slocum thought this should cheer him up.

Hector rode up beside him and whoa-ed his horse. He, too, took a look down into the sparse weeds. "Bled a lot," he said.

"Yup," said Slocum.

And then Hector took a second look. He scowled. "What the hell? Somebody join up with him?"

Slocum grinned. "Didn't you tell me that one'a those fellers you were looking for rode a gray that toed in?"

"Yeah, in the front."

"Well, our second man—the one what patched the first one up, looks like—rode in from the southeast on a horse that toed in," Slocum said, still grinning. "Course, I couldn't tell you what color he was . . ."

Hector nudged his mount a few yards to the south and peered down at the gravelly soil. "I'll be damned," he said softly. "Son of a bitch! It's the same fella, Slocum. I'd just about stake cash money on it."

For the first time since they'd ridden out of camp, Hector actually looked enthusiastic.

"Punk Alvarez," he went on. "That's the name they gave me. I'll be a ring-tailed tooter." And then he shook his head. "This thing's gettin' to have a kind of fated feel to it, ain't it, Slocum?"

"Either that," Slocum replied with a grin, "or you are the luckiest son of a bitch on the face of this earth."

"Either way's good enough for me."

They headed their horses out again at an easy jog, following the trail the two other horses had left in the thinning grass and the rocky earth. Whoever was in charge—and Slocum figured the wounded man wasn't in much shape to be, so it was likely this Punk character—wasn't too much in the brains department. He was making a beeline for Jaguar Springs, if Slocum was any judge. Hell, there was no place else to go out here, at least no place besides Jaguar Springs to find sure water.

Slocum had never been too fond of Jaguar Springs. There was water, to be sure, but on the occasions when he'd been near and needed it, he'd just nipped in, filled his canteens and water bags, and nipped out again. The cup of land where the spring welled up was too easy a place to get yourself ambushed, and the surrounding high rocks and boulders made the place pretty much a deathtrap.

It gave Slocum the collywobbles, if the truth were told.

But this lame-brained yahoo wasn't even going to the trouble of trying to disguise his destination. Now, if Slocum had been in his place and absolutely had to go into Jaguar Springs, he first would have cut down to the southeast to make sure of losing anybody on his trail. There was a broad plain down that way, carpeted in stone, that was made for losing track and fiddling posses. Punk had come from that direction, and would have had to know about it unless he was blind as well as stupid.

The only thing Slocum could figure was that Punk already had somebody chasing him from that direction, maybe from down around Tombstone. Men like him always had somebody or other on their tails. But then, he didn't seem in much of a hurry, either. The tracks were made by plodding horses, not racing ones.

Was it possible that Punk Alvarez didn't know that the man he'd helped had just escaped from a free-for-all shoot-out?

"Why ain't these boys hurryin'?" Hector asked, echoing his thoughts.

"You got me," Slocum replied with a shake of his head. "Can't figure it." He poked two fingers down into his pocket and pulled out his fixings bag. Creole was so steady-smooth at the jog that he could roll himself a quirlie and not lose a flake of tobacco.

He shook tobacco into the paper, rolled it, and gave it a lick. "You been awful quiet this mornin'," he said conversationally, as he poked the bag back into his pocket. He reached for a lucifer.

"Didn't get much sleep," Hector said, looking away.

Slocum struck the sulphur-tip, held it to his smoke, and inhaled deeply. "Coyotes keep you up?" he asked, shaking it out.

"Coyotes, my Aunt Fanny," Hector grumbled, and then he turned toward Slocum. "I wanna know how come it never changes."

Slocum arched a brow. "What?"

Theatrically, Hector threw an arm wide. "It's always the same damn thing. Whenever Slocum's around, there's always a beautiful woman. A beautiful sex-starved woman! And who always gets her every damned time? Slocum, that's who," he said without waiting for a reply.

"Honest to Christ, Slocum!" he went on in a rush.

"Remember that time when we was down in Mexico, clear out in the middle of nowhere? Along comes a lone coach, and who's in it? A goddamn countess, that's who. And a beautiful *French* countess at that! And that time when we was up in Montana, practically snowed in, and who comes stumblin' up to our door, half-froze to death and in dire need of bodily warmth?"

Slocum opened his mouth, intending to say that it wasn't *his* fault, but Hector cut him off before he could get a word out.

"That little blonde, Whatshername. The miner's daughter."

"Bathsheba O'Toole," Slocum offered.

"Whatever!" Hector shouted.

"Now, Hector . . . ," Slocum began.

"Don't say it, Slocum," Hector warned. "Don't go sayin' how you're sorry or it ain't your fault. I know damn well that you *are* sorry, and that it *ain't* your fault. And I also know that if the opportunity should poke its head up again—and I fully expect a stage to just wander across our path and a beautiful female in dire need of a good poke to fall out of it any damn second—you'd pounce on her like a duck on a June bug."

Hector shook his head sadly. "Once, just once, I'd like to be stuck out here in the asshole end of the world and have a beautiful woman show up, and have her turn her back on you entirely. I'd like to make you listen to me diddle her. Four times! Four times in one night, you bastard!"

All during Hector's tirade, Slocum had been biting the inside of his cheek to keep from laughing, but he couldn't hold it in anymore. It came out in a roar that brought tears to Slocum's eyes, and when he could talk again, he said, "Damn, Hector! If I'd known, I—"

"If you'd known I was awake by the fire, listenin' to Salty snore, oblivious-like, and that cowhand of his pretend to be asleep while he was playin' with hisself, you still would'a gone right ahead and diddled her, wouldn't you, you stinkin' reprobate?"

Slocum wiped a last tear of laughter from his eye and said, chuckling, "Well, I reckon you're right, Hector."

"Damn straight, I am!" Hector looked deliberately ahead through the frame of his horse's ears, and not at Slocum.

Still grinning, Slocum said, "Well, I'm right sorry. Didn't know you felt that way. Or that you were awake. Don't quite know how I can make up for that night of torture—"

"Six nights," Hector interjected. "Last night, two with the French countess, and three with that little blonde. Whatshername."

"Bathsheba O'Toole," said Slocum. The French countess had been redheaded and ripe and lusty as all get-out, but that tryst had also been over eleven years ago. All he could remember, insofar as a name went, was that she liked to be called *ma petite chou,* which somebody had later told him meant "my little cabbage." That was the French for you.

Hector grunted.

"Like I said," Slocum began again, "I didn't know you felt that way, Hector. Like to make it up to you."

"What you gonna do, Slocum, conjure up a female right here?" Hector said with a snort. "Though I wouldn't put it past you. Wouldn't put it past you at all."

Slocum chuckled softly. "Ain't no conjure to it. When we get to a town, I'll buy you—what did you say I owed you?"

"Six goddamned nights."

"All right. It'll pain me—and I think you're stretchin' it—but I'll buy you six nights of womanly companionship in the best cathouse in town."

Hector pivoted in his saddle. "Damn it, it ain't the actuality of it, it's the consarned principle!"

Slocum raised a brow. "Then you don't want six free nights of hoorahin'?"

Hector sniffed. "Didn't say that. I'd feel better about it if you were tied up in a chair on the other side of the wall, though. A real thin wall."

Having just precariously climbed down nearly forty feet from the top of a high boulder—and having sighted not a single, solitary soul traveling the vast, rolling expanse of land over which they'd come—Punk Alvarez was feeling pretty damned cocky. He figured they had got away free and clear. It wasn't a first, but it was close to it.

He slid down the last five feet, his hands pressed to the stone, the rock scraping his belly, and he lost a button. He bent and searched the gravelly soil for it, found it, and stuck it in a pocket to keep company with the one he'd lost in an earlier climb.

He was always losing buttons. It was the one drawback—besides the possibility of getting your head blown off every five minutes—of being a bandit on the owlhoot trail, and always having to climb or crawl someplace uncomfortable on your belly. Especially when a fellow had as big a belly as he had.

Of course, it beat the hell out of wearing a town suit and sitting behind a desk all day, or swabbing out saloons, or cleaning stables. Punk liked to think of the life he'd given up—not that he'd ever had it to trade—as a real refined one, though. He liked to think he was a smart fellow. He liked to think he might have been a lawyer or something if only he'd gotten past the second grade.

Not that he ever mention this to his companions. Punk was at least smart enough to know that lawyers weren't very popular with any of his compatriots. He liked to think he would have been a good one, though. He would have looked nice in a three-piece suit. He would have made quite a picture in his fancy office, smoking his expensive cigar. Punk had met a lawyer once, and had been impressed.

"Is it clear?" the man seated beside the dead campfire asked.

It struck Punk right about then that Cole Strait wasn't much taller standing up than he was sitting down. Not that Punk had much room to talk. Five and half feet tall, five and half feet around: that was Punk.

He said, "It sure is, Cole," trying not to be overly enthusiastic. The late, great Lando had always popped him upside the head if he got too eager about anything. Well, Lando getting himself killed just showed that God was watching, if you asked Punk, but he wasn't about to take any chances. Lando had popped him a few times too many before God finally did something about it. "I believe we lost 'em for good. How's your back?"

Cole moved a bit, then grimaced. "Hurts like sin," he said.

"S'pect it will for a while," Punk replied in a tone he hoped was sage. He squatted on his heels and poured himself the last cup of cold coffee. It tasted like shit and he supposed he should do something about building another fire, except that would entail leaving the shelter of Jaguar Springs to gather firewood. He wanted to be absolutely certain that nobody was trailing them before he did that.

"Any more of that?" Cole asked him.

Rats and piss. Now he'd have to snake out through the rocks anyway. He wanted to keep Cole real happy, at least until he answered Punk's question. He gathered his courage—mostly because he was impatient and he'd waited as long as he could stand—and asked it. "I'll get us another fire goin' in a minute here, Cole. But first, I wanted to jaw somethin' over with you."

Cole didn't reply, just raised his brows in a question.

"It's like this," Punk said, suddenly nervous. "I rode with Lando and Gordo, like I told you. And now I ain't got nobody to ride with for committin' banditry and the like. I ain't much good on my own," he admitted, "but I'm a damn fine back-up man. You could ask Lando. If he wasn't dead, I mean. And I was wonderin', since you're on your own, too . . . that is, I was wonderin' if we could ride together, you and me."

Cole started to say something, but Punk had wound himself up like a top, and there was no stopping him.

"See," he said, cutting Cole off before he got started, "you could figure out what mischief we'd get up to and you could give the orders, and I'd follow 'em. I'm good at followin' orders. Hell, I don't even care what we do. Stick up banks, hold up stages, rustle steers or horses, it don't make me no mind so long as I get paid fair and we get to a town every now and then. I fancy women and whiskey, same as anybody."

His top, once spinning wildly, ground down to a halt, and he just stopped and looked at Cole, blinking.

Cole cocked his head and said, "My goodness. You're sure a funny little man."

That comment made Punk a little mad, although he wasn't exactly sure why. But he didn't know what to say, so he just kept blinking.

Cole looked back at him a while longer before he said, "I think better with coffee, Punk."

Punk let out his breath with a whoosh. He hadn't realized he'd been holding it. Well, if an important man like Cole Strait wanted coffee—and he had said he'd think about taking him on, hadn't he?—than Punk supposed he'd best get to gathering kindling.

He sighed and stood up at exactly the split second

that Cole suddenly twisted his head to the west.

"Somebody's coming," Cole hissed, and motioned at Punk, motioned him back toward the rocks.

Punk was halfway across the little cup in the rocks before he realized that it couldn't be one of those boys who were chasing him—or not chasing him. He hadn't exactly made up his mind about that. But Cole had looked west, and that herd he'd rustled was northeast of them. Anybody following wouldn't have had time to get around that way.

He drew his gun and hid, nonetheless. He watched while Cole flattened behind the boulder he'd been sitting against, as the sounds of an approaching rider grew louder and louder. Whoever it was sure wasn't taking any pains to conceal himself from prying ears. And then the rider started singing some lame-ass song—"In the Pines, In the Pines, Where the Sun Never Shines," Punk thought it was—and Punk stood up and holstered his gun.

The singer was unmistakable.

Cole gestured at him, and for just a minute, Punk considered shooting the rider just to impress Cole. But to his credit, he said, "It's just old Gordo a-comin', Cole. Gordo Guardado. I told you about him, remember?"

And then he hollered, "Hey, Gordo! Get your sorry ass in here! You bring any firewood?"

15

At a little past noon, Slocum and Hector at last rode over the final rolling hump of the misnamed flatlands, and up to the edge of the freak rock formation, nearly ten miles around, that sheltered Jaguar Springs.

Reddish brown and yellowish boulders, huge ones, sprung up from the flats without preamble or warning. There were no smallish boulders or gradual change in the landscape to ease a man into it. Just those gigantic rocks thrusting from the gravelly soil like clenched and rusting armored fists.

The tracks had led them straight up to it, and now they led inside, through a narrow space in the stones that Slocum had always thought of as the Jaguar's Asshole.

"Wait a second, Hector," he said, and reined in Creole.

Hector complied, but tilted his head in an unspoken question.

"If they're still in there, we might as well just shoot ourselves in the head and get it over with. We ride in on 'em, and they'll have all the advantage."

Hector nodded grimly. "North or south?" he asked.

"They'll be watching to the north, if I'm any judge,"

143

Slocum said. "We'll go round, to the south. There's another entrance to the west. If they haven't come out that way, then we'll have to climb."

Hector craned his head up, and his face filled with dread. "Climb?"

"Hell, Hector," Slocum said dryly. "The highest places ain't more'n sixty, seventy feet."

Hector reined his horse to the south, and Slocum followed, chuckling softly.

They stayed close to the boulders, riding in their shadow for a while, and then into the sun. For over an hour they moved quietly, skirting the stony heights and not speaking, until at last they came to the western entrance to the hidden spring.

"That's funny," Hector said, and pointed.

Slocum scratched the back of his head. The fresh tracks of a solitary rider entered Jaguar Springs, but none came out.

"You suppose somebody met 'em?" Hector asked.

Slocum was already dismounting. He led Creole a few feet inside the passage in the rock so that he might have the benefit of its shade, but be tucked away enough to be hidden in case the three men snuck out past them. He didn't expect they'd try, but it was better to be prepared.

He pulled his rifle out of the boot. "Feel like climbin'?"

"Goddamn you, Slocum," Hector grumbled for maybe the sixth time. Each man had tied a latigo to his rifle, muzzle and butt, and they wore them across their backs to keep their hands free.

Hands? Raw stumps was more like it. Hector had taken the hide off his left palm before he remembered to put his gloves on.

They'd been climbing—and hopping, and inching,

and clinging for dear life—for nearly a half hour now, and they still hadn't sighted anybody. Of course, the pass through the rocks below wasn't always visible, but Hector hadn't seen anybody riding out the west end, either. He was beginning to think that they should have just gone in there, guns blazing.

He wouldn't have minded being shot so much as he minded being up here on this stinking hot-as-a-stove-lid rock, his boots slipping, his hand hurting like the devil, and the merciless sun scorching his back. No, after a half hour of this, being shot started sounding like a real picnic.

He tried to take his mind off it by wondering who the hell that third man was, down in there with the camel-murdering Punk. That got him nowhere, so then he tried to cheer himself up by envisioning those six nights Slocum was by-God going to pay for. All he could say was that they'd better get into a real big town with a genuine deluxe whorehouse.

He wasn't going to let Slocum get off with paying for six nights in a crib in some possum's butt of a mining town, no sir. It'd be champagne and silk sheets and fine cigars for him, not rotgut hooch and soiled rags for bed linens.

And after he finished up there, he'd take the money that Salty Nelson—or maybe Slocum—was going to pay him for this little adventure, and he'd buy him the nicest two-year-old colt he could find. Maybe a three-year-old, if the colt didn't have too many bad habits already. He'd raise him up nice, raise him up right.

There'd never be another Tico, but if he looked real hard, he might be able to find the next best thing.

He was thinking about this colt and had just about decided that if he had his druthers it'd be another bay, when he lost his tenuous grip on the rock and started to slither down.

"Slocum!" he hissed. It was almost twenty feet down to the top of the nearest boulder, and he didn't feel like climbing all the way back up. That was, if the fall didn't kill him.

He twisted his feet to the sides and tried to put on the brakes, but his boots weren't made for anything like climbing. They'd slow him down for a few seconds, then slip and set him free again to slither a couple more belly-grating feet downward.

He'd slid maybe ten feet straight down in this manner before Slocum inched close enough to catch his wrist. Just in time, too. The rock he'd been slipping down was about to tuck in at an angle, and his left boot caught nothing but air.

"Thanks," he breathed while Slocum hauled him over to the side, to a rock with a little footing.

Slocum just growled at him. "Quit horsin' around, Hector," he grumbled. "We got another half hour of this before we get to the rim of the cup."

Hector peered at his belly. The slide had scraped his shirt right through to the skin and taken a button with it. Another was hanging by a thread. "What cup? And you owe me a new shirt, goddamn it."

Slocum looked at him like he was a idiot. "The cup. The place in the rocks where the spring is."

"Well, how am I supposed to know you've got a pet name for every damn nook and cranny out here?"

The sun and the rocks were getting to Slocum, too, Hector supposed. It was like they were trying to navigate over hot, slippery skillets, and he didn't one bit care for the idea of himself as the bacon. He pulled his canteen free and took a swallow.

"Sorry," he said. "You want to name every cactus, it ain't my nevermind."

Slocum edged over to the right, which gave Hector a chance to ease himself somewhat. For the first time in fifteen minutes, he was able to put all his weight on his feet.

"How's your hand?" Slocum asked. "And I don't name every blamed cactus."

"You know what I mean. And it hurts, that's how it is."

"Ready?"

Hector stoppered his canteen and swung it back on its strap, over his shoulder. It clinked against the rifle and swung out wide above the chasm below.

Don't look down, Hector reminded himself. "Shit. I reckon."

"Cole Strait," Gordo said again. "It is the very great honor!"

Cole was ready to shoot the sniveling toadie, to shoot both of them. Punk, with his plans of following Cole on to some sort of outlaw glory, had been like fingernails on a chalkboard as far as Cole was concerned. But when you added this lummox into the mix . . .

"Cole Strait," Gordo repeated, and then he jumped up from his crouch, laughing, and slapped Cole on the shoulder.

Gordo was damn lucky it was the one that didn't have a bullet through it, but Cole grimaced just the same at the impact, hissing in air, and Punk dragged Gordo off to one side.

"You gotta stop that, Gordo!" he heard Punk say. "He done got hisself shot up, remember?"

"But he is someone famous, Punk," Gordo insisted. "I have never met a famous man before. Well, except for Emilio Vega, who was dead when I met him, and Silvestro Mondragon, who was also dead, and that son of a bitch Slocum, who I did not know was famous until after he was gone and the sheriff told me of his reputation. And I saw Wyatt Earp from a distance one time, but that was very long ago, before he was so celebrated as he is now. So you see—"

"Gordo?" said Punk, cutting him off.

"What, *mi amigo*?"

"Shut up, okay?"

Gordo shrugged.

Cole closed his eyes and swore softly. These two could have easily been models for a cartoonist's panel, the kind that magazines back east used to run, back when Cole had the time and wherewithal to read them. "The Adventures of Punk and Gordo, the Incredibly Inept Bandits," they might have called it.

They looked the part, too. Punk was short and fat— about as short as he was, Cole thought—and Gordo was just as fat, but about six feet tall, and with a big unkempt handlebar mustache to boot. If brains were gunpowder, both of them together might have had almost enough firepower to set off a single bullet. Individually? He doubted they could make a spark.

Punk had been pressuring Cole to give him an answer, to say right out that yes, he sure did want them to follow the trail with him. But Gordo had shown up in the nick of time, full of stories about his goddamn jailbreak. It sounded like so much dumb luck to Cole, but he let him keep on talking. At least it seemed to fascinate Punk and take his mind off other things.

He hadn't given Punk an answer yet, hadn't committed himself to riding with them—God forbid—because he figured Punk—and now Gordo—was just dumb enough to haul off and shoot him if he told them no. And either one might be lucky enough to kill him. Since Punk had taken his gunbelt before he slung him over his horse like a sack of corn, Cole wasn't much in the mood, or circumstance, to test this theory.

But the second he got his guns back, the second they got out in the open, he was heading south, to Mexico, money or no money. He figured he could always hold up a couple of stages on the way south. It wouldn't be the same as having herd money on which to start his new life, but it would have to do.

Conchita was waiting.

Despite Punk's having told Gordo to shut up, the two were still bickering. Cole rolled his eyes, then made a halfhearted attempt to move his shoulder. It hurt like hell, but he could stand it. He could ride. And he was already nervous about having stayed here so long. It had been quite a while since Punk had last climbed that rock and had a look back over their trail.

He grabbed a handful of granite and slowly pulled himself to his feet. Steadying himself, he called, "Punk!"

Punk wheeled around, a smile splitting his face. "You're standin'!"

Deferentially, Gordo took off his hat.

"Those water bags and canteens filled?"

"Yessir, Cole," Punk said, nodding rapidly, "they sure are."

"Then let's get moving."

Gordo moved toward the horses with all the speed of an elderly elephant, and Punk started gathering up gear. "We can ride together, then, Cole?" he asked while he snatched up the coffeepot and dumped it out over the fire.

When in doubt, lie, Cole thought, and said, "Why not?"

Gordo turned around about then, and said, "*Mierda!* You are one tiny *hombre,* señor! Punk, I think this one is even shorter than you!"

Before he thought to remind himself that he didn't have his guns back yet, Cole snapped, "I'm big enough to turn you inside out and take a shit on your innards, you big, fat Mex."

Gordo took an angry step toward him, but Punk

caught his arm. "He was only funnin', Gordo. He don't even have him a gun. Wasn't you funnin', Cole?"

Gordo appeared to be cooling rapidly, but Cole was still boiling. "You insult me again, and you'll get worse than words. Understand?"

Apparently Cole still had his old air of military command—or Gordo wasn't quite as stupid as he'd first thought—because Gordo's only answer, after a moment, was "Fine." And then he turned and slouched back to the horses.

Punk leaned toward Cole. "You don't wanna go pissin' him off, there, Cole. He ain't too bright."

It was the pot calling the kettle fire-scorched, but Cole didn't think it was the time to comment. He'd spoken in anger, and one of these days it was going to get him killed.

But Gordo had touched his one sore spot, which was his height, or lack thereof. All through the war they'd called him General Tiny or Colonel Dink behind his back. They'd called him worse names when they threw him in prison for trying to make off with that gold shipment. And they'd called him far worse yet—although he hadn't imagined it were possible—in the years since. And each time, the anger he felt had quite literally made his vision blur.

Well, that was almost over. He'd get shed of these jaspers as fast as he could. He'd head south. And he'd stay there.

Nobody called him names in Paso Pedregoso, by God.

"Which way we goin', Cole?" asked Punk. The horses were saddled, loaded with water, and ready to go.

It didn't make much difference. Gordo offered Tombstone as a happy option, but Punk proudly offered, "Anyplace 'cept Tombstone. Got a couple'a fellers lookin' for me down that way."

He'd already shared the story of his night with the singer with Cole, who was not amused.

"And it can not be Pozo Artesiano," Gordo added. "The sheriff there, he is looking for me, also. Did I tell you of my daring escape?"

Cole sighed. "Twice. Anyplace you boys ain't wanted?"

The two looked at each other and shrugged.

Actually, Pozo Artesiano would be a prime place for stocking provisions and heading down into Mexico, to Paso Pedregoso. So he said, "I've got business in Pozo. What say you two fellers head on over to Mexican Wells and wait for me."

Nobody said anything, so Cole, patience wearing thin, rephrased it. "Anybody here wanted in Mexican Wells?"

Punk and Gordo looked at each other and shook their heads.

"All right," Cole said. "Then that's the plan."

But a look of something resembling distrust passed briefly over Punk's eyes. Haltingly, he asked, "How 'bout if ol' Gordo goes on down to Mexican Wells? I'd admire to tag along with you, Cole. They got women in Pozo Artesiano. I ain't wanted there—leastwise, no more than anyplace else."

Cole kept his face pleasantly blank. "Sure," he said. He supposed that if Punk was too hard to shake, he could just shoot the singer-raping son of a bitch. Anybody tried that with his Conchita, they'd be dead before they got a hand to the first button on their trousers.

He smiled. "That'd be fine."

Slocum and Hector edged slowly forward. They were now within inches of sight of the camp, and if they came out where Slocum remembered, they'd have the position not only to take those boys out—if they didn't just give up, that was—but also to get back down to the ground.

The trip back to claim their ponies would take a fraction of the time on foot.

He signaled to Hector to get ready, and then he slowly eased around the edge of one of those giant boulders.

It was the place, all right.

Nobody was there.

"Shit," he spat. "Son of a bitch!"

"What?" whispered Hector. He crowded closer and peered down twenty feet, to the empty cup. "Goddamn it!"

"Back," said Slocum, and gave him a none-to-gentle nudge in the ribs. "Back around there until you can see somethin'."

"See what?" Hector said, backing as fast as he could.

"Till you can see over to the east, damn it!" Slocum was himself navigating his way to the south, edging along the outside of a big round boulder, trying to see to the west. If those boys had flown the coop completely . . .

"I see 'em!" called Hector, and Slocum turned just in time to see him brace his body against the rocks, and brace his rifle against his shoulder.

Hector fired once, then twice, then slowly lowered his rifle. Slocum couldn't see what he was firing at for the rocks in his way.

"What?" he said as he edged closer.

"Three of 'em, all right," said Hector. He looked a little pale despite the heat shimmering off the rocks all around. "Two headed due east. Too far for me to throw lead at. And one headed southeast. That one, I got."

Hector hesitated then, and Slocum said, "What else?"

"You ain't gonna like it."

"Hector . . ."

"The two goin' east had our horses."

16

After they skittered down in the cup and filled their canteens, Slocum and Hector exited the rocks and started southwest, toward the body. Hector had spotted the man's horse grazing not too far away, and one horse between the two of them was better than none.

Besides, Slocum wanted to see just who it was that Hector had shot, if only to give the body a good kicking. The gall of this shitheel, stealing his horse! All right, he hadn't exactly stolen Creole, but he'd been a party to it. Slocum didn't forgive easy when it came to horseflesh.

A little over an hour after Hector fired the shot, they finally walked, stiff-legged, up to the body. It was quite obviously dead. The flies were already buzzing thick on the exposed skin.

Besides, Hector's bullet had made quite an exit hole in the man's chest.

They both stood there in silence, staring down at the bloody corpse. And then Hector thumbed back his hat and said, "How in the blue Jesus you suppose he busted out of Ploughshare's jail?"

Slocum shook his head. "Son of a bitch stole my horse *twice*! I mean to have words with Bill Ploughshare when we get to Pozo."

"Words?" said Hector. "I'd hate to be wearin' his badge right about then . . ."

Between the two of them, they managed to catch the late Gordo's horse, which was understandably spooky, and Slocum went through the saddlebags.

"Well, Gordo thieved this one, too," he said, holding out a fan of letters. "Addressed to one Ben Hoflin. There's a *BH* tooled into the saddle skirt, too."

Hector turned back toward the distant corpse. "You been a real bad boy, Gordo," he scolded.

Slocum swung a leg over the chestnut. "Let's get goin'. That is, unless you want to bury the bastard."

"Leave him for the coyotes," Hector replied as they started westward, Hector walking off Slocum's flank. "And I don't recall flippin' a coin for the first ride, Slocum."

"Didn't flip one."

"Seems to me you should have. After all, you was the one what left our horses up there. Practically had a sign on 'em that said 'Steal Me.' "

Slocum suddenly reined in the chestnut and glared down at Hector. "I've left horses in there a couple of times before, and nobody was ever the wiser, you smartass son of a bitch. It was that goddamn nag you borrowed from Salty, I'll lay money on it. The bastard likely wandered right off his ground tie and came creeping around that rock, and those two that got away saw him. Creole stays put on a ground tie."

"You don't need to be so touchy."

"I ain't touchy!"

Hector shrugged and started walking again. "All right, you ain't touchy. I still say it was your fault."

Slocum squeezed the horse with his knees and it leapt up beside the walking Hector. It still had plenty of run in it, that was for sure. Slocum said, "Hold up."

Hector stopped, and so did Slocum. Slocum took his

foot out of the near stirrup. "Get up, damnit."

Hector obviously knew better than to say anything. He stuck his foot in the leather and clambered up behind Slocum, who started the horse walking again before Hector was all the way settled.

"Pozo Artesiano?" asked Hector.

"Looks like," said Slocum, and urged the chestnut into a soft jog.

Far ahead, Punk and Cole were switching horses. Cole didn't think there was much chance that they were being followed—at least, followed very closely—but he figured to make all the time he could.

His luck was turning, he was sure of it. No sooner had Gordo ridden out of the rocks and kicked his horse into a gallop, headed south to Mexican Wells, than Punk had hollered at him to come take a look-see.

Gordo was long gone by that time, but when Cole turned his horse around, he found Punk just grabbing the reins of a sorrel gelding. And when Cole investigated further, he found a real nice Appy gelding, ground tied back in the rocks. He'd snagged that one, and they'd taken off toward Pozo.

He'd heard the shots, just barely, and had looked in time to see a far-off Gordo topple from his galloping horse. And all he'd thought was, *One down, one to go.*

It wasn't until they stopped to switch horses that Punk said, "Y'know, I do believe that's the same horse what Gordo stole a couple'a days back. I mean, how many Palouse horses do you see out here, anyway?" He stuck a thick finger up his nose and dug around. "Never liked 'em much, myself. Don't trust a horse with a white ring around his eye."

"This is the horse he got caught for stealing?" Cole asked, and looked away. He had shortened the Appy's left stirrup, and now he moved to shorten the right. The horse's previous rider had been very tall, which predisposed him to dislike the man, even if the man hadn't been shooting at him.

And then something buzzed into Cole's consciousness. He hadn't really been listening to Gordo earlier, but now a name rose to the top of his brain. "Did he say the fellow that caught him—when he stole this horse, I mean—was called Slocum?"

Punk nodded. "That's it. The same feller what owned the horse. Reckon he's back there right now, shank's mare." He laughed.

Cole didn't join in, though. Could this Slocum possibly be the one he was thinking of?

No. That Slocum had been young, wild, and deadly, and drew trouble to him like lamplight drew moths. That Slocum would have perished years ago, likely at the wrong end of a bullet or a rope.

Cole stuck his foot in the stirrup and hoisted himself up on the Appy. Punk mounted, too, and gathered his reins.

"That was sure something back there with ol' Gordo, weren't it?" Punk asked conversationally.

For a moment, Cole wasn't sure what he meant. He wasn't entirely sure that Punk had seen Gordo fall, and they had been too busy galloping to speak until now. He hadn't mentioned it because he figured Punk would get upset, he and Gordo being pals and all. Not that Cole much cared how Punk felt, one way or the other, but a shook-up man was liable to travel slower. And a lot crankier.

"Which?" Cole asked. Punk might mean that Gordo had joined them at all. After all, breaking out of jail was Gordo's first so-called miracle, and running into them was his second.

"You mean to tell me that you didn't see Gordo get shot?" Punk asked. He swung a hand into the air, palm out flat, and laughed. "Went flying, just like that. Deader'n an iron stove, I reckon."

If Cole had been feeling the tiniest bit bad about his inevitable murder of the nose-picking Punk Alvarez—which he was not—this single comment would have quelled any doubts he had on the matter.

So he just said, "Let's go," and sunk his knees into the Appy.

They rode off west on the two reasonably fresh horses, trailing the spent ones behind.

At nightfall, Slocum and Hector stopped and made camp. Slocum planned to get off his aching feet, for they had ridden, then walked, then taken turns riding. And once he got some hot grub in his belly, he planned to set out again. He didn't know what ol' Hector planned on doing, but Slocum was taking the horse with him.

The dead man's stolen horse was laden with full saddlebags, and Hector whipped them up a pretty fair supper and a pot of coffee.

"You figure they'll cut the Appy loose before they hit Pozo?" Hector asked over his third cup of coffee.

Slocum helped himself to more skillet biscuits. "If they've got half a brain betwixt 'em," he said. "Gordo must have recognized him."

Hector chuckled. "Bill Ploughshare'll shit a brick if he sees that ol' horse of yours come into town under another new rider. Reckon he's peeved as all get-out, what with losin' a prisoner."

Slocum thought about the sheriff of Pozo Artesiano, arrow-straight and sticky about such things as rules, and nodded in agreement. He'd bet that Bill was fit to be tied, all right. He'd also bet that Bill wasn't at the jail at the time of Gordo's break-out. Probably one of those new deputies of his, who was now—if Slocum was any judge—officially not a deputy anymore.

Slocum sort of hoped that Gordo had been stupid enough not to recognize the horse, and that those two yahoos would ride straight into town with him. Bill Ploughshare'd be on them like a half-starved duck on a fat June bug, and save Slocum and Hector a whole lot of trouble.

Maybe some gunplay, too.

Suddenly very serious, Hector put his coffee cup down. "Back there," he said, staring out into the darkness.

It was all he needed to say. Both he and Slocum stood up and backed away from the fire, out of its circle of light. Slocum could hear it now, too. Horses approaching, at least two.

They had backed in opposite directions and Slocum couldn't see Hector anymore. He had likely crouched down in the weeds, and Slocum did, too, his gun drawn and ready. You never knew who the hell you were going to meet out here.

Most of the time they weren't any too friendly.

The sound of plodding hooves stopped before he could see anyone, and there was a long moment before somebody hollered, "Hello, the camp! Anybody build that sorry excuse for a fire, or did the Lord God burn Hisself another bush?"

Slocum draped the hand holding his Colt over one knee and grinned. "That you, Salty?"

He heard a snort, then, "Can we come in, you possum's butt, or are you gonna shoot us?"

Slocum stood up and holstered his pistol as he walked toward the fire, calling, "What the devil you doin' out here? You're supposed to be up north, mollycoddlin' those beeves."

Two horses neared the fire. Hector, who had joined Slocum, squinted hard into the darkness and said, "Goddamn your ornery hide, Slocum! I knew it, I just *knew* it!"

Connie Nelson jogged ahead of her uncle and into the fire's light. "Knew what, Hector?" she asked as she slid to the ground. She was looking at Slocum, though, and there was a great big grin on her face.

Salty Nelson rode in right behind her. "Pushed 'em up toward the ranch, Slocum," he said, oblivious. "Figured the boys could do the rest. And then this one," he said, poking a thumb toward Connie, "decided to get all worried about you, seein' as how I figured to have about half-killed that last rustler. What I mean to say is that you didn't come back right off, draggin' a carcass."

Slocum only had eyes for Connie, and she was looking pretty damn good, too. He glanced at Salty, then back at Connie, and said, "Nice'a you to think of me."

"My pleasure," said Connie with a wink.

"Got kind of worried about you when we seen all them tracks goin' every which way around the spring," Salty went on. "What the hell happened, anyway? And who was that buzzard bait you left back there? Was it my last rustler?"

"All in good time," said Hector as he took Salty's reins from him. He slid a glance toward Slocum. "Or bad time, depending on how you look at it."

"You folks eat yet?" Slocum asked.

"Well, we was just strippin' the tack off these horses when we saw your fire," Salty said, and his teeth gave a little click. He pointed to the east. "We was way the hell off over that'a way. Looked to us like you lost your horses back there, Slocum. Like you're makin' do with just one."

"That we are, Salty." Slocum said. "Glad to see you. Be even gladder if you had an extra mount along, though."

Salty laughed. "I just bet you would. So what's the

deal? Looked to us like that damned rustler found a buddy."

"Why don't you fill each other in?" Connie offered. "I can help Hector with the horses and listen at the same time."

"Nice'a somebody to think of me, too," Hector groused from the edge of the light.

Slocum started from the beginning, and within ten minutes had Salty—and Connie—pretty well squared away on the situation. "I figured to set out again tonight, once we got supper taken care of," he added.

"Aw, shit," groaned Hector, who was just sitting down across the fire. Connie came, too, and sat beside Slocum, bumping him, purposely, with her hip.

Hector continued, "I have spent half this damn day walkin'! I was countin' on restin' my dogs for the night."

"We ain't goin' nowhere till I eat," Salty said firmly. He stared at their skillets, which still contained two whole biscuits and the remains of Hector's chicken stew, which he'd made from the tins he'd found in the saddle-bags. The stolen horse had been well stocked, indeed. There were tinned peaches for desert, too, although Slocum hadn't gotten that far.

Hector said, "Well, I reckon Mr. Ben Hoflin can spare the grub."

"Who's Ben Hoflin?" Connie and Salty asked as one, which entailed some more explanation from Slocum.

Hector got to work opening cans and Connie got to work, too, fixing more biscuits and a fresh pot of coffee, while Slocum rolled himself a quirlie. They weren't going anywhere for a while, that was certain. He was glad for the company, though. Not that Hector wasn't an able conversationalist, but Connie was sure a lot prettier.

"We found somethin' strange up there, Slocum," Salty said.

Slocum arched a brow.

"When we was rounding up strays in No Man's Land, I mean," Salty continued. "Down in this little sinkhole— and I mean little—we found us a dead rustler. Skull was crushed. The mud was all churned to hell, and we figure there was a few cows caught down in there and he was tryin' to get 'em out."

Slocum waited for the rest.

"One'a the hands found his horse—least, we think it was his horse—walled into a makeshift stall out there in the rocks. Somebody'd put a bunch of brush across a hole in the rocks and left it there to die. We come across it in time, but tell me, who'd do a thing like that?"

Slocum didn't have to answer.

"The late Lando Reese, that's who," spat Hector.

17

None of them got much sleep that night. None, that is, save for Salty Nelson, who snored almost nonstop in his saddle as the rest of them alternately rode, then led, the horses westward over the trail left by their quarry. The sky was clear, the moon was close to full, and the trail disappeared from time to time, but between Slocum and Hector they kept on course.

"Don't know why we're botherin'," Hector said as the horses tramped around yet another patch of prickly pear. "Those owlhoots are going straight to Pozo, no doubt about it."

"You'd feel real dumb if we galloped into Pozo and found out later that they'd veered off someplace out here, Hector," Slocum said. Connie was riding behind him at the moment, her head heavy against his back, and he spoke softly so as to not wake her. "And I'd be pretty damn pissed off."

"Wouldn't mind that," Hector replied. "Just like to get to a hotel and a bed."

Slocum grunted. "Thought you were all fired up about gettin' those camel killers."

"Got two of 'em. The thrill of it's wearin' off."

163

They stopped at ten o'clock, by Slocum's watch, and then again at one in the morning, to rest and water the horses, and also to grab a little shuteye for themselves. Never long, though. Never for more than a half hour. And at each stop, Connie was transferred to Hector, or back to Slocum again.

"I'm beginning to feel like Pass-Around Patsy," she grumbled at four, when they remounted again. This time, she was going up behind Hector.

"You should," remarked Salty, who seemed to finally be awake for the day.

"Good morning to you, too, Uncle Salty," Connie said. "And I'll ask you to keep your wisecracks to yourself." Her mouth set into a line, and she hauled off and slugged the smirking Hector in the arm. "You, too," she growled.

Slocum, who had seen Hector's shoulders shaking while he held back a laugh, took the wiser road and said nothing.

Hector grunted at the blow, but kept his mouth shut, too.

At roughly five-thirty, when the sun was just peeping over the horizon and the desert was painted with an eerie dawn light, Slocum held up his hand and halted the small group of riders. He swiveled in his saddle, pulled his spyglass from his saddlebags, and took a look.

"What is it?" Connie asked. "What do you see?"

Slocum didn't answer for a second. First, he popped the spyglass with the flat of his hand, collapsing it, then shoved it back into the saddlebags.

"My goddamn horse," he said curtly. "Yours, too, Hector."

"It's Salty's, really," Hector muttered as he pulled his Winchester free of the boot and checked the magazine. "I just borrowed it."

"Whoever it belongs to, it looks like those fellers just

turned 'em out," Slocum said. "They're out there grazing. Just got their halters on, with the lead ropes draggin'. Don't look like they're hobbled, either." He turned toward Connie. "Get down," he said.

She tightened her hold on Hector's middle and stuck her pretty nose in the air. "I won't."

"You will," Slocum said sternly. "Now, Connie."

"I will not," she started to say, but it rapidly turned into a cry of *"Hey!"* when Hector turned and gave her a shove.

"Sorry," Hector said matter-of-factly once she was down on the ground. "Ain't got time to fight with you."

"Salty, you stay put. And make sure that she does, too," Slocum said. And before either of them had a chance to argue, he sank his knees into the horse. Hector was right behind him.

Cole saw the brief flash of light from Punk's mirror. They were coming. He signaled back just as quickly, and hoped Punk had the sense to put that mirror away. It'd be just like him to keep flashing it, probably right at the two riders.

They'd taken the bait, and were cantering straight toward him. Punk was across the plain, maybe three hundred yards away and crouched, as was Cole, behind a thick stand of prickly pear. This particular area was rife with it, and they'd had no worries about places to secrete themselves. Their own horses were tethered out of sight in a shallow wash, a short way down the broad plain.

He peered through the crotch of a couple of cactus pads. They were riding closer, but they'd slowed down to a jog. Suspicious. They should be, seeing as how they were riding into a deathtrap.

Cole, unlike Punk, didn't like to take any chances, and he'd figured that those boys would be madder than all get-out. He'd also figured that they'd follow, and all the sooner if they could catch Gordo's horse. In fact, he'd counted on it. Of course, he didn't figure they'd catch up to him quite so soon. They must have traveled straight through the night.

They were bullheaded as well as single-minded.

Well, fine. That kind could die just as dead as any other.

They were in range now. He brought up his rifle and seated its butt loosely against his shoulder, waiting for them to come in far enough so that he and Punk could get them in their crossfire.

"C'mon," he whispered, "c'mon . . ."

They were taking their own sweet time. They were down to a walk. Two big men, both dark. He couldn't tell much more.

"C'mon," he whispered again. Sweat that had nothing to do with the cool morning trickled down his nose.

He heard one man whistle, soft and low. The Appy's head came up and it started ambling toward the whistler, its lead rope swinging lazily. Of all the stupid luck!

But the other nag grazed, oblivious. They'd have to come in to get that one. One of the bastards would, anyway.

He pressed the butt of his rifle stock into his shoulder and stared down the sights.

The riders started forward again. One man headed for the Appy, who had closed the distance between them by half, and the other rode out for the chestnut. They were separating, but that was all right. Or would be, if Punk would just hold his damned water.

But Punk didn't. Suddenly, a shot pierced the stillness. The riders jumped off their horses and dived for cover. Punk fired again and again, and the riders returned his fire.

But Cole had the presence of mind, in that split second, not to fire. To the sound of rifle shots, he eased his gun down and watched.

Let them kill Punk. It would save him from doing it, he reasoned. Let them kill Punk and take their goddamn horses and go on their way.

He made a furtive movement toward the gully where he'd secreted their mounts, then stopped himself before he'd moved an inch. Stupid. Wait and see.

"Slocum!" he heard somebody call. It sure wasn't Punk.

A second voice called, "You get him?" and Cole's blood ran cold. It couldn't be. Not after all these years.

The first voice said, "Sure looks like. He ain't breathin' or nothin'." And then the man stood up. He was clear over where Punk was supposed to be—where he still was, as far as Cole knew—and kicked at something on the ground. He looked back across the plain and shouted, "This here camel murderer's deader'n a hammer."

"Where's the second man, Hector?" Slocum called. He was still crouched down in the grass, and Cole couldn't see him. "And for God's sake, get down, you idiot!"

"There was only the one shootin' at us," Hector shouted back. "Mayhap they had a fallin' out." Then he turned the other way and stared to the southwest. "See what you gone and done, you sorry-ass camel killer?" he asked Punk's corpse. "You spooked my horse to hell and gone. Ought to shoot you again, just on general principle." He gave the body another kick.

And then Cole saw Slocum slowly stand up, a rifle swinging from his hand. He was still too distant to make out the details of his face, and he was more fleshed out in the body than Cole remembered, but that was natural, wasn't it? He hadn't seen Slocum since the war. He'd been just a raw-boned kid then. A nosy kid who saw and heard too much, and then had the brains—and the gall—to put two and two together.

Slocum started away from him, toward Hector and the body.

If it was the same Slocum—and Cole was convinced it was—then he couldn't count on them taking their horses and leaving. Just the opposite. That goddamn Slocum would likely poke all around the area, turning up his and Punk's mounts. Turning up him.

He couldn't have that.

The Appy had wandered within thirty feet of his hiding place behind the prickly pear. A shame it couldn't have been one of the others. Gordo had said that this was Slocum's horse, but it couldn't be helped. As he began to work his way toward the Appaloosa, crouching low, his butt bumping his heels, he told himself that he could dump the Appy in the first town he came to. He still had enough cash in his pockets to outfit himself, and the Appy would bring a good price.

It'd be better if he just went straight south once he traded horses, better if he didn't try to make up the cash loss—the loss of the herd—by holding up a stage or two.

"Easy, you wall-eyed broomtail," he whispered as he neared the Appy. He chanced a quick peek over the brush, and saw that Slocum's back was turned, and the other man, Hector, was even further out. They were both walking away, toward the errant chestnut.

"Easy, easy," he said, and snagged the Appy's dangling rope.

He stayed crouched low, though. The horse was big to start with, and a whole lot taller when a man didn't have a stirrup to help him hop on. Especially when a man was as short as he was, and as over the hill.

Over the hill. He'd never thought about it in exactly those terms. Why it should come to him now, when he was hunkered down in the weeds and cactus, about to try to ride a horse bareback for the border with that smart son of a bitch, Corporal John Slocum, on his trail, was a mystery.

He reached up slowly, keeping the horse's body between himself and the distant Slocum, grabbed a handful of mane, and with a Herculean effort, managed to mount. He hadn't ridden bareback in a coon's age, and when he sank his heels into the horse's sides and the surprised gelding bolted off, Cole nearly lost his seat.

Not quite, though.

He bent low over the horse's whipping mane and spurred him to the south, deeper into the desert.

18

Hector had just put a hand on the chestnut's halter rope when Slocum wheeled at the sound of galloping hooves.

Creole!

"Shit!" he spat, grabbed the chestnut away from Hector, and leapt onto his bare back. "Not *again*!"

"You'll never catch him on that one!" Hector shouted. "Take the bay!"

Slocum didn't waste time answering. He wheeled the chestnut and spurred it toward the bay Connie had been riding—and which he'd relieved her of.

He didn't take time to dismount, either. When he neared the other horse, he leapt from the chestnut's bare back and into the saddle of the startled bay. One thrashed rear later, he was galloping after Creole and the miscreant who had stolen him. He was beginning to think that horse was jinxed.

Creole was fast, a lot faster than Connie's bay, but Slocum figured Creole was laboring under a strange rider. That rider was also traveling without a bridle and saddle, and appeared to be having a little trouble hanging on.

Slocum coaxed all the speed he could out of Connie's

bay, and began to gain a little. He knew damn well that
Creole, if he'd been trying, could have run rings around
him. Thank God the joker riding him couldn't seem to
grip Creole's slick sides for more than a half second in
the same place. Several times Slocum saw a flash of
silver as the man tried to spur Creole with one of those
wildly swinging boots, and missed.

Actually, he was sort of hoping the numbskull *would*
spur him in just the wrong place. Creole was funny. He
was just about the best horse that Slocum had ever
owned, but if you even nudged him with a rowel—high
on the flanks, almost to his hip—he'd just quit whatever
he was doing and start crow-hopping like crazy. Luckily,
it wasn't any place a man could spur without being half-
contortionist. You could touch it with a curry comb, and
Creole had even been known to react to that.

Slocum was closer now, almost close enough to shoot
worth a damn. He rose a few inches out of the saddle,
balancing on his feet and his knees, his weight over the
horse's withers, and brought up his pistol. And in that
same instant the horse thief must have realized he was
in peril, because he twisted around and fired a shot at
Slocum.

Slocum felt something sting his ear. The thought that
this jasper was one hell of a marksman—or just impossibly lucky—had barely had time to flit over his mind
when, up ahead, Creole stumbled.

The rider didn't lose his seat, not yet. But from what
Slocum could see, he flew up in the air, still clinging to
Creole's mane. His legs went out behind him. He
bounced once, belly down, on the galloping horse's
back, and then somehow managed to pull himself back
to something resembling a sitting position. But on the
way to righting himself, he ran his spur over Creole's
bad spot.

All hell broke loose.

Creole stopped running and started to buck like he'd never been broke in the first place. His rider went flying in a big hurry, hit the ground, and rolled clear of Creole's heels. Slocum put the brakes on fast, and vaulted clear of his mount while it was still trying to slow down, and while the other man was still rolling.

The bay, suddenly relieved of a rider, lazily cantered on out, reins flapping. Creole just kept on bucking. Now hidden in the brush, Slocum tried to figure out where that horse thief had gotten off to.

He didn't have long to wonder. The horse thief knew where Slocum was, all right, because just then another shot clipped off brittle twigs to the left of Slocum's head.

Slocum returned the fire, rolled, and fired two more rounds toward the source of the first shot, but he was firing blind. The vegetation was spotty here, but it consisted of waist-high sage and creosote. Two men could creep around out here for days and never see each other.

Creole had finally stopped his tantrum, and there was no sound except for his heavy blowing and the thin whine of the breeze through the brush. No sooner had the thought come into Slocum's mind that Hector had best stay back if he knew what was good for him, than he heard rapidly approaching hoofbeats.

Silently, he cursed himself blue. He could either wave Hector down and keep him from getting blasted—and thus show the horse thief exactly were he was—or he could let Hector draw the man's fire, and get himself a good bead on his quarry.

It took Slocum exactly a half second to decide which option he'd take. He'd drawn Hector into this mess, and he wasn't about to let him get shot for his trouble.

He sprang to his feet, ready to wave the rapidly nearing Hector away. But at the same moment the horse thief had risen, too, and was drawing a bead on Hector.

Surprised, the man had only begun to spin, to change his target to Slocum instead, when Slocum fired his Colt. The horse thief got off a shot as well, but he was already falling and it went wide of the target.

Hector reined his horse to a rearing halt and vaulted off his horse, into a crouch. He cupped a hand to his mouth and called, "You all right?"

Slocum waved a hand at him.

"He dead?"

Slocum shrugged, and signaled Hector to circle around to the west. He bent low, and began to creep toward the place where the horse thief had gone down. And all the time that he was working his way through the brambles and brush, something kept nagging at him.

When at last he reached the man, that "something" crystalized. The man was sprawled on the ground, his pistol near his outstretched fingers, but he was still breathing. Slocum kicked the gun away, then knelt to him.

"Strait," he said grimly. "Major Cole Strait. Always wondered what happened to you after you busted clear of that prison."

Strait was obviously dying, and Slocum bit back the urge to spit on him. During the war, Strait had been his commanding officer for a short time. Short, because Slocum had overheard Strait and his henchmen making plans to steal the gold shipment they'd been ordered to guard on its way to headquarters.

Slocum had turned Strait in. Strait had gone to prison, but had escaped before they got a chance to execute him. Captain Hawkins, Strait's second in command, was captured in Louisiana and hanged not a month after the escape. The third man in his party, Lieutenant LaTour, was shot off a galloping horse in Texas four years later. Nobody had seen or heard from Cole Strait again.

And now here he was. Still stealing after all these years. Some men never learned.

"Well," said Cole Strait. The word came out of him in a little bubble of blood. "If it isn't Corporal Shitheel Slocum." He coughed up more blood, and Slocum lifted his torso up a little. He was a tiny man, very light, really no more than the size of a boy.

"You all right?" Slocum looked up to find Hector standing over them, rifle in hand. "Your ear's bleedin'," Hector said.

"You are one quiet son of a bitch," Slocum replied. He felt at his ear. It seemed to be all there, but his hand came away bloody, all right. Then he looked back at Cole Strait.

Cole's eyes had lost any semblance of focus. His head lolled back, and with one last burble of dark blood, he whispered something. Slocum leaned in to hear.

"What?" asked Hector as Slocum closed Cole Strait's eyes. "What'd he say?"

Slocum stood up. "Conchita."

"What's that supposed to mean?"

"I don't know," Slocum said as he stared down at the corpse. Poor little son-of-a-bitching bastard. A man takes a wrong step somewhere along the way, and it changes the whole course of his life. "Maybe she was who he was riding toward."

"Here comes the cavalry," Hector said, and Slocum looked up to see Salty and Connie Nelson heading their way at a jog, and leading the rest of the horses. Creole's saddle had been hurriedly tied on top of another horse's tack, and it threatened to fall at each step. The horse bearing it didn't look any too happy about the extra stirrups flopping around, either.

"I'll go pick up your bay," Hector said, "and when I get back, you can tell me what we're gonna do next."

*   *   *

They arrived in Pozo Artesiano after nightfall, and dropped Cole Strait's body, along with Punk's, at Bill Ploughshare's office. Sheriff Ploughshare immediately sent for the undertaker, and while they waited for him, Ploughshare gave Slocum and Hector a voucher for six hundred dollars in reward money.

"Gotta go over to New Mexico to pick it up," he drawled, "but I reckon that much money's worth the trip. New Mexico's where they been hangin' out the last few years, though I never heard'a them ridin' together before." Bill shook his head. "Cattle, horses, same-old same-old for Strait. Before that, it was Texas, but their paper's pretty yellow. Don't know if they'll still pay on it. And course, Punk's wanted for murder. This is all you're gettin' out of me," he added. "Already paid you for Gordo. Who, by the way, I ain't goin' out to pick up."

They joined Salty and Connie for dinner. Connie was freshly scrubbed and wearing a pretty blue dress that she bought after she convinced the mercantile's owner to open up after hours. She looked good enough to eat, and Slocum planned on having her for desert.

She was hungry for him, too, if busy hands under the dinner table were any indication.

"Reckon we'll be getting back east come morning," Salty said over his enchiladas.

"Now, Uncle Salty . . . ," Connie began.

"Don't you 'now' me, girl," he said with a little click of his choppers. "We stay any longer, and there's no tellin' what mischief you'll get up to."

She didn't say anything, just sat there grinning.

Slocum knew exactly what kind of mischief she was planning, however, and so after supper he practically ran up the street to Paolo "Muy Malo" San Francisco's cat-house, hauling Hector along.

The house was jumping. Muy Malo himself was banging out Chopin on the piano—one of the few whore-house pianos in Slocum's experience that was actually in tune—and the parlor was full of men waiting their turn.

Slocum shouldered his way into the parlor and held up a hand. *"Hola!* Muy Malo!" he shouted over the din.

"Slocum!" Muy Malo gleefully shouted back, never missing a note. "You come back so soon! You must like our ladies very much, no? Graciela! Maria!"

Two girls appeared at Slocum and Hector's sides.

"Take your pick, Hector," Slocum shouted over the piano and the loud talk. "I ain't stayin'."

Hector looked over the buxom Graciela and the slim, athletic Maria, and said, "Both of 'em."

Graciela rubbed up against him, and Maria gave his ass a pinch and giggled.

"Both?" asked Slocum with a sly smile. "For six days? I ain't made of money, y'know."

Hector grinned, thumbed back his hat, and settled an arm around each girl. "Two of 'em for three days, then."

"That's fair, I reckon."

When Muy Malo finished the piano piece, Slocum thumbed off bill after bill and handed it over, consid-erably depleting his half of the money from Salty. But his word was his word, and he kept it.

When he walked out the door, Hector was climbing the stairs with a big grin on his face and a girl on each arm.

Connie slipped into his hotel room not five minutes after he got there.

"Uncle Salty's tucked up for the night," she said, smiling. "Teeth in a glass and sawing wood."

"That's nice," Slocum said, and kissed her.

They made love on a soft hotel bed, wild and frantic at first, then sweet and slow. Connie must have been quite the moneymaker in her day, he thought idly, when they were between rounds. She was eager, she was fiery, but she had a sweetness, a sort of soft core beneath the tough exterior, that was incredibly appealing.

And her body, of course. Breasts like firm, ripe melons, tipped with aureolas the color of pale salmon. Her skin was flawless and milky, not a single mole or freckle.

He knew. He'd seen every inch of it here in the hotel. He took his time about it, too. On this occasion, he had the luxury of four walls around them and lamplight by which to study her.

Her waist was tiny and her hips slim, but rounded. Her legs were long and shapely—longer than fashion would approve of, but the kind men like him wanted wrapped around them. Delicate hands and feet, thick, wavy hair that swung nearly to her waist, and a face that could launch a thousand ships—and had undoubtedly launched quite a few awe-struck cowboys—completed the picture.

At the moment, she sat opposite him, naked and cross-legged at the foot of the bed. A thin skin of sweat glistened over her curves, and she was smoking the quirlie he'd rolled for her. It was all Slocum could do to keep his eyes from the open juncture of her thighs.

He thought he'd better. It was only polite, after all.

Well, the hell with polite.

"You're quite a man, Slocum," she said, and blew smoke out through her nostrils. "Might be that it's just been a long time for me, but glory! Nobody ever made me come the way you do."

Being naked and having no hat to tip, he grinned and touched his brow. "My pleasure, ma'am. Completely. You're quite a woman."

She smiled. "I know." She gestured toward the bottle

of champagne he'd talked Muy Malo into selling him. "Any more of that?"

He picked up her glass from the nightstand, poured a few frothy fingers into it, and handed it to her, then poured one for himself.

She lifted hers in a toast. "Here's to that big, fat pecker of yours."

He grinned. "I'll drink to that."

"And the man behind it," she added, then drained her glass. "Looks to me like you're ready again, you nasty thing."

"That's me, all right," he said crawling toward her.

As he took her in his arms, turned her, and bent her over the high foot rail, she whispered, "I've got to talk Uncle Salty into sticking around town for a few extra days."

"Three, at least," Slocum said, cupping his hands over smooth breasts, feeling the hard little nipples drag against his palms. "Damn. Connie, did I ever tell you you're gorgeous?"

"Yes, but you can say it again," she said, reaching back between her open legs to wrap her hand around his thudding cock.

He dipped his head to kiss the back of her neck. "You're gorgeous."

"And you're inventive," she hissed when he slid into her, then pulled her back onto his lap, seating himself even deeper inside her.

He slung an arm about her waist and began to rise up into her, his free hand caressing her beautiful back, then her breasts, then her back again.

She moved with him, lifting, then sitting down hard, grinding and circling her hips in perfect rhythm to his thrusts. Her hands clutched the top rail of the foot board in a white-knuckled death grip as she pushed back into him, and soon he recognized the little sounds she made, the sounds that signaled she was about to climax.

He slid his hand down to her sodden curls and briefly slipped a finger lower to touch his cock, thrusting in and out of her. And then he found her secret nub of flesh, now swollen with passion. He very lightly skimmed his fingertip over it, and was rewarded when her heard her suck in air, through her teeth.

Suddenly the tingle in his own loins turned into a bright roar, and just before he felt himself go over the edge entirely, he stroked her again.

She froze, tightening her internal muscles, and milked a sudden—and tremendous—orgasm from him. They both made noise, he was fairly certain, she in a low, breathless moan and he in a grunting groan. And after a moment, after their muscles relaxed, while they were still tingling and slick with sweat and washed in the afterglow, they both flopped back on the sheets.

"You'd better stay," panted Slocum.

"At least three days," Connie breathed. "Jesus Christ."

Three days later, halfway to Tucson and a long way from New Mexico, Slocum and Hector waved goodbye to Salty and Connie. Salty was feeling fit, having had his choppers adjusted by the dentist in Pozo Artesiano, a man he claimed was far superior to the tooth-yanker in Tucson. Slocum figured he was right. Salty's teeth hadn't clicked once, nor had his thumb gone into his mouth to adjust his upper plate.

Connie looked as relaxed and sated as Slocum felt, and Hector looked, well, worn down to a nub. A happy nub, though.

As they watched Salty and Connie head slowly northeast, leading the string of dead men's ponies, Slocum said, "Thought you were gonna buy a colt."

"Didn't see one I liked," Hector replied. "And there

wasn't much time to look around. I was kinda busy, what with Muy Malo's gals and all."

Slocum grunted. "Maybe there's a good one in New Mexico. Salty give you that horse you're ridin', or you buy him?"

"He's on loan," Hector said, patting the sorrel's neck. "I'll drop him off once we pick up our reward money and I find my new colt."

Slocum stared at Connie's back as she disappeared into the distance. "Maybe I'll just ride back with you, then."

Hector shook his head and grinned. "You never change, do you, Slocum? Course, I imagine it'll be a good spell before we get back this way."

Slocum arched a brow. "Why?"

"Because of all the trouble you're gonna draw on the way there and back, of course. I swear, you catch inconveniences the way flypaper catches flies."

"Inconveniences?"

"I'm tryin' to be nice. It's better'n sayin' shitloads of trouble."

"Hector?"

"Yeah?"

Slocum grinned. "Shut up and ride."

With a pair of rebel yells, they fanned their horses into the east—toward New Mexico, money, and glorious new inconveniences.

Watch for

SLOCUM AND THE RANCH WAR

280th novel in the exciting SLOCUM series
from Jove

Coming in June!

JAKE LOGAN
TODAY'S HOTTEST ACTION WESTERN!

LONGARM

Explore the exciting Old West with one of the men who made it wild!

J.R. ROBERTS
THE GUNSMITH